Puffin Books

GHOST IN THE WATER

It all started when Teresa and David discovered the curious inscription on a gravestone in the local churchyard: *In Memory of Abigail Parkes. Departed this Life 10th December 1860. Aged 17. Innocent of All Harm.* It was these last words – *Innocent of All Harm* – which excited their curiosity.

Then Teresa found an odd relic of the dead girl, and the hunt was really on: the two children were determined to find out more about Abigail, and particularly about the mystery of her sudden death. How could they know that the dead girl's life was strangely linked with Teresa's own, and that Abigail's weary spirit would not let them rest until they had come to a clear understanding of the mystery?

Edward Chitham has woven real places and actual events into his unusual novel in which the mystery and surprise of the story are set against a vivid background of the streets and canals of the Black Country.

D1448621

Edward Chitham

GHOST IN THE WATER

Puffin Books

Puffin Books, Penguin Books Ltd, Harmondsworth, Middlesex, England
Penguin Books, 625 Madison Avenue, New York, New York 10022, U.S.A.
Penguin Books Australia Ltd, Ringwood, Victoria, Australia
Penguin Books Canada Ltd, 2801 John Street, Markham, Ontario, Canada L3R 1B4
Penguin Books (N.Z.) Ltd, 182–190 Wairau Road, Auckland 10, New Zealand

First published by Longman Young Books 1973
Published in Puffin Books 1982

Copyright © Edward Chitham, 1973
All rights reserved

Reproduced, printed and bound in Great Britain by
Hazell Watson & Viney Ltd, Aylesbury, Bucks

Author's Note

This story is set in and around Rowley Regis and Old Hill in the Black Country. Many of the places described are quite real, and some of the incidents really happened. But if anyone recognises himself or herself in the story, he or she has a vivid imagination. There was no coal mine near Slack Hillock called Fiery Holes, and anyone who tries to walk along the the towpath through Gosty Hill canal tunnel is in for a surprise.

Contents

Innocent of all Harm

It was a dark, blustery night, I remember. Rain was slashing across my face and wetting my straggly hair, which had no covering on it, because of the school rules. These state that the only kind of hat girls can wear is a beret. The churchyard was pitch black, and we kept falling over iron edgings and catching hold of slimy gravestones to stop us falling. I really thought the whole thing was mad; and we dursn't use the torch because the battery was low.

'Have you got the notebook?' David asked.

I fished in my school bag and out it came, but I couldn't see to open it and the rain was sploshing down from the trees.

'I can't see,' I told him. 'We'll have to waste some of the torch. Have you got the slightest idea where we are?'

'I'm almost sure it's near here,' said the little swot boy. 'It's with some others the same age.'

I switched the torch on and found the page. A blob of rain trickled down my nose on to the pencil writing and smudged it.

'There's Cutler, Loveridge, Edwards and more Parkeses round it,' I said.

'Thanks,' said the swot, taking the torch and shining its weak beam on the graves all round. He had to go within a foot to see the writing.

'I've got a Cutler,' he said, his voice coming muffled through his scarf. His mother always made him wrap up well these cold days, and I could just see the outline of his heavy coat bending over the grave. I wondered again what had made me come traipsing up to the church on such a rotten night. I knew my mom would call me a drowned rat and get quite wild. And I was supposed to be home hours ago, and she might be a bit worried, really. I had a conscience about it.

'Get a shift on, do.' I shivered.

'I've got it!' came the reply. 'Find the page and I'll read it to you.'

'We know what it says anyway,' I answered. 'And I've got the page. I've had it ages. It's sobbing wet by now, with half a gallon of water on it.'

'I'll read the gravestone, then you can check on the list,' he said.

'Yes, do. But for Holy Moses' sake get a move on.'

'*In Memory of Abigail Parkes*,' he read. '*Departed this Life 10th December 1860*. That's all, I think. Not much cop.'

'Well, I told you it didn't prove anything. There must be hundreds of Abigail Parkeses. Anyway, pass the torch over. I can't see.'

'Wait a bit. There's some more. A bit lower down. It's her age!'

'Well, if so, we must have missed it out last time, because I'll swear it's not in the notebook.' We had been pretty rushed when we did the copying before; we could have missed bits.

'*Aged 17*,' David read on. 'And what's this mean? *Innocent of all harm*. It looks funny writing to me.'

'What the hell are you on about, "Innocent of all harm"?' I asked. 'Really, it never says that?'

'It does, though,' he answered.

I looked, and it did. *Aged 17. Innocent of all harm.* Well, I knew that wasn't in the notebook, and when I checked I was right.

'It's not down here,' I told him. 'I suppose we're not seeing things?'

'Well, look again.'

So I looked and looked in the fading torchlight. There was no doubt at all about the wording, though we had to hold the torch about three inches away from the stone to read it. I don't honestly know if the writing looked different or not, because of the light. It might have been the same kind of lettering as the first part. Just then the torch went out and I looked away into the blackness, seeing the faint yellow words 'innocent', 'innocent', 'aged 17', 'of all harm', dancing in front of my eyes.

I wasn't the least bit excited by our discovery. Instead, I felt cross and stupid. I was mad with David for bringing me up there and mad with myself for coming. It was as if he was a conjurer who'd tricked me into seeing something which wasn't there. I just couldn't believe that I'd missed those words when we'd been writing down the gravestones, and if I had I was wild with myself for my carelessness. The whole thing seemed foolish and depressing.

Climbing off the hump of the grave, David sprawled on the slippery path; it was all over moss and he fell quite flat.

'Oh, get up,' I shouted. 'Can't you look where you're going?'

Of course he couldn't. It was as black as Gosty Hill canal tunnel. Then suddenly I realised I was being jolly unfair to the lad. He hadn't fallen on purpose, and his idea of coming up to see the grave had certainly paid off. What it meant, I had no idea, but at least he'd been right to come. So I helped him on to his feet. There was nothing I could do about the muddy smears I guessed he had on his coat; I couldn't see them, so I couldn't get them off. We hurried back to the road, where at least there were street lights. For some reason we were both keen to be out of the dark churchyard, and it wasn't till we stood outside the main gate, under its swaying lamp, that we could talk.

'There can't be any mistake, you know,' said David.

'No,' I answered. 'And I just can't understand how I came to miss those words the other time. I suppose it looks as if I must have.'

'Unless some joker put them there since,' he laughed.

As I stood there on the sodden footpath with the wind wrapping my wet coat round the back of my legs, I didn't feel like laughing. The page in the notebook was suddenly whisked away by the squally gale and I had to play tick with it in the middle of the road before I could catch it.

'I'm going home,' I said. 'And quickly.'

At the bottom of it was our form's local history society. Form 2a had been copying all the graves in the churchyard. Some were quite old, back to the eighteenth century. This history society met every now and again after school to see how we'd all been getting on, and to start new ideas going. Some people say history repeats itself, others that it's 'bunk'. I only know it's fascinating.

Earlier on that wet and windy autumn day the few people really interested had met. I'd brought an interesting object, as we sometimes did, if we could find anything. It was a trade token my dad had found in the vegetable plot. Another person had collected all the names on the canal bridges from Windmill End to Station Road. Someone else had found part of an old mineral railway, with the lines still whole, though rusty. In days gone by, these mineral lines used to shift coal from the pits to the canals or the iron works, and dinky little trains used to run on them, with overhead cables.

Tracy Dobbs brought a sampler. Samplers are odd things, and we don't have them nowadays. But a hundred years or so ago, girls used to have sewing lessons instead of learning Latin and Maths and all the brainy things the boys were learning. They used to embroider pretty designs, flowers and things, on a piece of cloth, with a text or a proverb or a line of poetry. Then if it was nicely done, they'd frame it and hang it up. They put their name and age on too. There are a good many of these samplers still around if you look.

'We've got one at home,' I told Tracy.

'You would have Teresa Willetts, a clever thing like you,' she said. At times Tracy can be very offensive.

'It's not as big as yours,' I said, ever trying to be peaceable. 'And I don't think it's as pretty, really.'

David Ray was standing just by. He is a small clever boy with floppy dark hair and specs. In the past we have been somewhat thrown together because he is interested in things, not just gossip. Of course, he knows too much, and I doubt if he's human, but you can get used to him—to quite like him, in fact. Mind, he doesn't care for football, which is against him. Naturally, I support the Albion myself, the greatest team out.

David said, 'I didn't know you'd got one, Teresa. Is it old?'

Why should he think he knows everything I've got? Even Val didn't know, and at the time she was my best friend.

'Bound to be, I suppose. It's hanging in our hall. Somebody called Abigail did it. I ask you, what a name!' It is strange that I scoffed at the name, because secretly I liked it, and thought of calling my first girl child that, if I was going to be married ever, which as a matter of fact, I'm not.

'I saw that name when we did the gravestones,' David answered. 'It's in your notebook, I think.'

We didn't have time to look at the notebook there and then because our form teacher came in and the meeting started properly. I enjoyed that hour. The teacher talked about these mineral railways I mentioned. He had a lot of pictures of them, and kept telling us we could find out new things about local history too. I'm very pleased we have this local history society. Some of the girls are only there to hang round the boys, of course, but some are really keen, and personally I think the past is marvellous. You can really live it, when you hold these old objects in your hands, or see the old pictures. I love history, I do.

As we moved out of the classroom, after the meeting had finished, David Ray came up to me.

'Have you got the notebook?' he asked.

'I'd forgotten.' I said. I felt I'd like to be sweet to him, really I did. But he is so persistent if he gets an idea in his head. I honestly hadn't remembered old Abigail, but he must have been letting her simmer, you might say, at the back of his mind during the meeting.

I got the notebook out, and we turned it up. '*In memory of Abigail Parkes, departed this life 10th December 1860,*' I read out. 'Not very exciting at all.'

'Doesn't say much, does it?' he agreed.

'But now I come to think of it,' I put in, 'I do believe our sampler is Parkes as well. Isn't that odd?'

He seemed to think a bit. 'Shall we go and see if we can find it again?'

I thought of saying 'What for?' but I did see the possibility that it could be the same Abigail Parkes as on our sampler at home, and I was intrigued by the coincidence.

'I'd somehow like to see the grave. I wonder if it could be the same one. There doesn't seem to be any age on the gravestone.' He peered seriously from behind his glasses.

'It's absolutely pitch dark,' I told him. 'I hope you've got X-ray eyes.'

'No, a torch, it's better,' he smiled.

He never told me the torch battery was nearly worn out, and I never thought how wet and dark the night was, or how silly it would feel to go out of school with David Ray and walk along the lane with a puppet boy muffled to the ears in half a blanket which he called his scarf. If I had thought, I wouldn't have gone. And now I'm glad I did, though I wasn't till a long time after.

The wind more or less blew me home that night except when it blew me away from home. The church is set high up on a steep hill, and as I hurtled down the village street I hardly seemed to be putting my feet on the ground at all. Halfway down the hill David left to go his own way and to think his own thoughts. I had no idea what they might be, except that they'd surely be something clever.

Across the valley thousands of street lights were twinkling in the rain. You could see straight lines of them marching over towards Dudley—red orange they were—and clusters of them down in Old Hill, with here and there the red neon light of a pub or the searchlight beam of a moving car. The Black Country's not supposed to be pretty, but at night with all the shimmering lights it's enchanted. I love this view from the hill, with the valley a sparkling earthbound milky way.

When I got to our garden gate and felt for the catch the wind blew my hair across my eyes, and in brushing it away I let go the gate which banged with an almighty thump against the palings. At the same time the dustbin lid flew off and careered along the path, ringing out like the clashing shields in an ancient battle. When I was smaller it used to make me jump a mile, but I'm used to it now, whenever the wind tears through our council estate.

The front door opened and a light shone out before I reached it. Mom's voice shouted, 'Who's there? Is that you, Teresa?'

'Yes,' I shouted, but no one could have heard above the wind.

'Teresa? Is that you? Oh, good. It's about time you came . . . Oh! You look like a drowned rat!'

I pressed on towards the door, and we banged it behind us. There was something in the hall I wanted to see. Of course, I was glad to see Mom too, but I was after the sampler. Unfortunately I had no chance to get near it.

'Up you go and change straight away. You're dripping! Take your shoes off at once, and dry your hair on the towel. There's one on the towel rail in the bathroom.'

'Just a minute, Mom. Could I just . . . ?'

'Now do what I said. I don't want you with one of your coughs. I haven't got time to be nursing you.'

So it was five minutes or so before I came down to have a good look at the sampler. I felt much more comfortable of course. It is amazing how often parents are right when they seem to be a nuisance.

I jumped down the last few steps and sprawled on the hall floor, almost as flat as David in the churchyard. No one seemed to have heard so I stood on tiptoe squinting at the sampler in the dull light of our hall. Since we had the concealed lighting put in you only want piped music to make it like a Chinese restaurant! Of course, the light reflected off the glass in the front of the sampler and all I could see was an image of the kitchen door. I got a chair.

'Whatever are you doing now?' asked Mom suddenly, coming out of the front room where I could hear our telly booming on.

'Looking at the sampler,' I answered cagily.

'Well, your tea's just about frizzled. I put your baked beans in the oven when you didn't come home. I wonder I bother to cook anything for you.'

'I won't be half a minute,' I said.

'You can get your own beans when you've a mind,' Mom answered tartly, and went back to Z Cars or whatever it was.

I gently lifted the sampler off its picture hook and put it on the floor. Now at last I could read it:

A B C D E F G H I J K L M N O P Q R S T U V W X Y Z

Cast your bread upon the waters.

Let him who is without sin cast the first stone.

Where your treasure is, there shall your heart be also.

Abigail Parkes   Aged 11   A 1854 D

The writing had an interlaced pattern of dark green round it, and there were some red and some yellow letters. The yellow and red formed flowers too, in places, like the flowers of gorse. The green twisted round the rest, sometimes dense and dark, sometimes with spikes like gorse spikes, that really looked sharp and prickly. The embroidery cotton, or wool, or whatever it was, still showed up brightly against the grey-brown background, which looked like some sort of canvas.

I stood looking at it for some time, trying to hold it so that the light shone on it. The floor was still the best though, because whenever I stood up the light shone on the glass, and I couldn't read it. When I thought I could remember it, I put it back on the wall and got the dried-up beans out of the oven. I took them into the front, where Dad and Mom were lapping up the telly, and for a bit I was jerked back to the present. This was a pity, because I wanted to think, and before I could do that I had all my homework to do.

My bed was big and empty when I finally got into it. The wind was still moping round the house and rain pelted at the windows so that I thought it'd break them. I curled up, away from the wind and my Maths homework, and tried to think about this Abigail.

Now suppose I was doing a story about her in an English

lesson. I'd start with the funeral. There'd be a slow procession with high-stepping horses, going up the steep village street. They'd all be in black, sad and gloomy; and the polished coffin would be carried shoulder high through the lych gate to its eternal resting place. I could imagine the crowd of mourners reverently doffing their hats as the clergyman read the final prayers. I could see weeping uncles and aunts . . .

But then suddenly I abandoned this line of thought as a clearer picture came into my head, sharp in focus. The time seemed to be suddenly 'now', not 'then'. The wind sighs, no longer raging. It is a grey winter day. The red-brick church is gone from the top of the hill, and I feel as if I am standing beside a grey stone tower; the rest of the church is also grey and brown stone. The trees are vanished from the churchyard, leaving the place bare, and the gravestones cluster thickly up to the church. I glance to the lych gate, but it has gone. Instead there is an ordinary farm gate, and by it stands a cart. The single horse is puffing and sweating from the climb up the hill. Two men are nearby, undoing the fastenings to let down the tail of the cart. I can see the coffin on the cart as they do so.

Looking round towards the church, I watch a clergyman coming down the path. He is carrying a book, and his face looks truly sad and perturbed, not with the mock sadness of most clergy at funerals. He walks to the gate nervously, as if slightly wary or reluctant to do what he has to do.

'Good afternoon, Mr Ward, sir,' I hear one of the men say. He is a prosperous looking, black-suited man of middle age. The face beneath his top hat is worried too, not just grieving. He keeps looking round, as if he feels guilty.

'This way please, Mr Parkes,' says Mr Ward. 'It will be as well to make haste. The rain, you know, can hardly keep off for long.' Then he leads the way while the two men

carry the coffin up the graveyard to the waiting hole. I
know its location all right, though the churchyard is grimly
bare.

As for me, I am so muddled that I hardly dare go on with
my imagining; though, on the other hand, I can't stop.
The party goes out of earshot, and I don't know if I can
bear to overlook their privacy. I still seem to be standing
close in against the grey church wall, but they never notice
me. Am I imagining these people of the nineteenth
century, or am I, Teresa Willetts from the 1970s, only an
insubstantial wraith? Which are the real people in the
churchyard, and which the shadowy intruders from another
age?

I hover by the church, frightened to go nearer the grave
in case they accost me and ask me what I want. I listen to
the service read by Mr Ward, while the prosperous man,
top hat in hand, gazes into the earth. The third man
throws earth on the coffin. Now they come wearily back
down the path.

The funeral is over, but another person comes up the
churchyard, a young dark-haired man, respectably but not
expensively dressed. Instead of merely gazing at the new-
made grave he kneels down, puts on it a home made posy of
December wild flowers, gorse, wild roses and evergreen.
What a truly Victorian gesture! A green and blue sadness,
more vivid than waking, takes hold of me. With a fearful
struggle, I tear myself away. The picture vanishes, and I
sit up in bed shivering slightly to drink a glass of water
before snuggling back under the clothes; and this time
I sing myself quietly into a calm sleep, without dreams.

2
Beginning of a Quest

The next morning was Friday. Val and I caught the school bus, for once, and sat downstairs. Now, I thought Val was my best friend. She used to be. But I've noticed the last year she isn't quite on the same wavelength. She shows off, she teases and taunts, she's always chasing the boys. I don't care what she does, but she will keep favouring me with her advice all the time. Worthless, silly advice it is, and it'll drive me mad. This time I just couldn't listen to her. She was on about the Maths homework, which didn't hold much charm for me. I'd slaved hours over it last night, and I was for giving the subject a rest.

'Oh, shut up,' I heard myself say. 'Let the dead bury the dead. I mean, that's last night's worry.'

'This morning's, mate,' Val insisted. 'I keep telling you. I couldn't do it. How about a lend of yourn?'

'Well, now I know you're saft, our Val,' I answered. 'Kingy'll spot that ten mile off.'

'I won't copy, honest,' she replied, wide-eyed. 'Only I want to get some ideas. Go on, Tess. I haven't got a clue, me. Anyway, how did you get yourn done? I'll bet swotty Dave did it. I know you went to local history.'

'All right, so I went. But he never did my Maths, that's for sure. Hacked out by the amateur Willetts brain, that was.'

'I bet Dave went home with you.'

'He did not then, so there. Only to the churchyard, to look at a grave,' I added, honesty or something prompting me.

'A grave?'

'You know, a gravestone.'

'Well, it's you that's saft, Teresa. And hopeless. Quite beyond it, you are. I suppose you always have been really.'

'Thank you, I'm sure . . . Look here, Val. There's something odd about one of the graves. Can I tell you about it?'

And I was just going to do so when the bus reached school, and I had to concentrate on getting off without being squashed to death in the crush. It's a good job this happened, because I know now that Val wouldn't have understood. This does seem to happen, that you have a friend for years, then suddenly something comes up which makes a little wall between you, and you can never go back. I'm afraid she did borrow the Maths homework, though, and did get us both into trouble. As for Abigail, she had to wait till break when I saw David Ray.

David is not all that gain with his hands. He spilt his milk that morning as he was getting it out of the vending machine. It went all over my shoe, and I think he apologised; there was pretty much of a racket going on at the time. I felt terribly shy of telling him my theory about Abigail, my new theory that had come to me that morning. Was it ridiculous? Did it fit, exactly? True, there was a lot to suggest it . . .

We both spoke at once: 'I was thinking about the queer gravestone . . .' 'I've been thinking about Abigail . . .' we said, and broke off suddenly, full of confusion.

'You tell me first,' I said encouragingly.

'No, ladies first,' he answered.

I looked for the tinge of mockery you often get when a boy says that, but it was quite absent. The lad really meant to be courteous, and I felt honoured by the courtesy.

'Well,' I began. 'You've got to say that even if you count the extra words the inscription's short. It makes me think there's something odd. I mean, where's the "In loving memory of . . ." or "Dearly beloved daughter of . . ." that you'd usually get? That kind of thing's a must on Victorian graves. Then, I was dreaming about Abigail's funeral last night. It came to me that it was a poor miserable little funeral, when mostly people had rather grand ones in those days, even if they couldn't afford it. Perhaps Abigail was very poor.

'Well, look. What about that sampler? Did it say how old it was?'

'Yes, it did. It said she was eleven in 1854.'

'Well, there you are. Seventeen in 1860. It must be, Teresa. And a poor girl'd never have time to stitch a sampler. Mind you, it is a bit of a coincidence, but it must be the same one.'

'A poor girl wouldn't have the money to stitch a sampler, anyway.'

'No. She'd be shifting coal or making bricks according to our history teachers. Oh, perhaps the sampler doesn't come into it after all.'

'I think it does,' I answered. 'I'll tell you what. I think either the family fell on hard times, or else there was something funny about Abigail's death. I suppose she wasn't murdered?'

'Well, she wouldn't be any the less beloved daughter and all the rest if she'd been murdered . . .'

'What do you think of suicide?' I asked, letting out my theory. But, oh dear, I didn't want such a tragic end for the poor girl.

'Mmm . . . There was a time when suicides had to be buried at crossroads. Even in 1860 I'll bet they'd be buried in an unhallowed place. Not in the churchyard . . . or not in the main part of the churchyard, I should think.'

'And what about the "Innocent of all harm"?' I asked.

'Yes. I want to know where that came from. I'd like to see it in daylight. so there can't be any error.'

'Do you really, David?'

'Get off!' he shouted. I jumped with surprise, but then realised he wasn't talking to me. Someone had nearly knocked his milk out of his hand. The someone, a large lad with close-cropped hair, stepped back on to David's foot.

'Sorry, but I meant it,' he said.

'Do I what?' David asked, shouting to be heard above the row.

'Do you want to find out any more? I mean, I've got this idea running round my head that perhaps there's something funny about this girl's death. I'm just keen to know what.'

'Yes. Me too. We might find out who she was at the church. The parish register might say something about her death. And there should be a death certificate, too, somewhere.'

'It seems an early age to die. I'd hate to think I'd only got another three or four years.'

The thought of my elder sister came to me; she would be the same age as Abigail.

'I suppose seventeen is her real age?' David asked.

'It agrees with the sampler all right.'

'But still,' he continued thoughtfully, 'that's the age people ought to start living, not dying. Though I feel quite alive now, actually.'

He looks alive, with his sharp eyes twinkling through his glasses. I suppose it's a funny kind of alive though, to be a walking encyclopedia and not care about football or music. All the music he cares for is Bach and that sort of thing, and I must admit that's frightening!

'I know the vicar, you see. We could go tomorrow morning and ask him.'

I couldn't quite believe my ears. He was apparently cutting me in on a Saturday morning visit, and I thought it very kind of him. I wouldn't exactly have called him 'my type' of person, but the expedition sounded a bit better than just traipsing down the shops with Val. And as I say, David and I have sometimes been thrown together a bit in the past.

'That sounds a good idea . . . I'm right with you,' I nonchalantly replied.

And so it was fixed. This was where our quest started, the quest for a long dead girl whose uneasy spirit—if that was what it was—wouldn't let us rest until we knew every-thing, and who led us through darkness and confusion, and me through real danger, to clear understanding.

3
In the Churchyard

I woke up the next day feeling I'd just had an interesting
dream, but couldn't remember it. Our Jean—my elder
sister—was fast asleep in her bed. The lazy devil never gets
up till late of a Saturday. She goes to the Tech. on Friday
on day release, then she lets her hair down on the night,
so you can't get her up in the morning. I looked out of the
window.

The rain had cleared up overnight, and I thought we
might have a dry mild day. I remembered I was going on
this mad expedition to the church, raking up the dead;
then I tried to visualise meeting young David out of school
uniform, but I just couldn't picture it. I needn't have
bothered; when he turned up it was in the same old blazer
and grey trousers he wears every day. Over the top he had
his floppy coat and the blanket he calls his scarf.

As for me, I chose some red jeans and a bright green
cardigan, as different from school uniform as possible. I
fiddled with lipstick, goodness knows why, then splodged
it all off again. Why put on lipstick to meet the dead? I
shut the door very quietly, leaving the sleeping beauty
lying there like an embowered princess, and stole quietly
downstairs to a ghastly smell of burnt toast. It wasn't
Mom either, it was the electric toaster. The sampler hung
in shadow, looking quizzically at me, but I took no notice
and banged into the kitchen.

At the appointed hour I was standing by the bus stop at
gorgeous Blackheath market. I hope to work there one day

—not for good, I hasten to add, but for a Saturday and holiday job. Mom fusses about it: is it quite genteel for a grammar school girl to work in a market on Saturday? Perhaps not, but who cares anyway? It's the only way to get money, working for it. You can't expect parents to slave at jobs all week for luxuries for their children when their children get to teen-age. By that time, a bit of self-help's wanted.

The red bus drew up with a bump, and parked so as to block the main road. The driver tried to shove the folk off the bus as quick as he could so as to have a quick smoke, but it took him twice as long as it need have because he was parked right up against a car and they had to squash between the car and the bus like meeny mice. People do the first thing that comes into their heads, though. This driver just stopped when he felt like it instead of looking a bit further and saving himself trouble. So, what with shopping baskets and trolleys and pushchairs, it took a long time for David to appear.

When I saw his rig-out I was bitterly humiliated, really I was. I just couldn't bear to look at his long grey trousers, his scruffy school tie and his old balnket. What a mercy he hadn't got a cap on! And I suppose he could have been wearing that too, so I must be grateful for small things. But truly, I had no business to feel shamed; the lad had a perfect right to wear what he wanted. His dark eyes peered seriously at me from behind his glasses, and of course I had to forgive him. Half a bar of Cadbury's Dairy Milk also helped.

'I think we ought to ring up first,' he said. I'd never thought of it, but of course he was right. You can't just barge in on vicars, they've got plenty to do.

We queued outside the phone box, then squeezed inside. I don't use phones very often, and the red smallness of the box added to my confusion in using this one. Luckily

David dialled as I watched, and almost at once the owl-eyed boy was speaking to a smart-voiced clergyman up the hill.

It was quite clear they weren't strangers. I could hear the voice at the other end being quite matey in its tones, and the boy at this end got excited. The vicar was on about weddings, not funerals. I realised he meant weddings now, this morning, which would be using the vestry to sign in. David's negotiations continued. If we got there very quickly indeed, we could take the books we wanted over to the vicarage to look at. Then we could go into the vestry after the weddings were over.

'So we must get a shift on,' said the boy, putting down the phone.

'We'll have to run,' I answered.

We alternately ran and walked, and made it in less than twenty minutes, but it was a dreadful grind. We couldn't talk. David's running was more like scurrying, but he covered the ground all right. Anyway, I'm not in the Olympic class myself, so I can't talk. But even with all this haste, we were too late, as I'll explain.

My eyes were swimming as we neared the top of the hill. I could hear my heart thumping, and I felt a little bit sick. Outside the lych-gate stood what I at first thought was one of the wedding cars, but as I blinked and screwed up my eyes, I could see it was a horse-drawn cart, the tail being let down by a rough looking carter, while a dignified man in black stood waiting by the side. I clutched David excitedly; he was looking only at the ground as he fought with the dreadful hill which has buses stalling and pedestrians slipping any frosty day in winter.

'Hey! Look!' I tried to utter, but my hoarse voice wouldn't cope with the words, and I only squeaked.

I forced my head up to look at the waiting cart again. Some lengthy object was being taken from the back. I tripped and my shoe fell off.

'Oh, cuss!' I said. 'Wait for me.'

'What are you talking about?' asked David, as he slowed down. 'Look at what?' So he had heard the gist of the squeak.

'Look at the cart,' I panted. 'Quickly. What can you see?' I badly needed his confirmation. I thought I knew what the cart was. I had seen it before, in my dream on Thursday night.

'Cart? Car, did you say?'

'Cart,' I screeched. 'By the lych-gate. Can't you tell me what it's like? Quick, while I get this blamed shoe on.'

'It's one of the wedding cars,' he answered. 'And you're quite right to panic. I'm afraid that means we've missed the vicar. He'll be busy with this for ages now.'

'It's never just an ordinary car?'

'Not quite ordinary. It's an old Daimler,' he agreed. 'They should have sold it to a museum. It'd fetch a good bit by now.'

I simply banged my foot into the wretched shoe and squinted again. Of course, David was right. It was a Daimler wedding car, and I was completely taken aback. Even through all the sweat and fuzziness of the climb, I was sure it had been a cart there. Naturally, it couldn't have been. That was quite obvious to me as soon as I thought about it. I'd thought myself in the last century, or the last century here and now, or something. That made twice in one week. At the time, I felt no surprise at Abigail's coffin being carried off the cart; my only surprise was now, when I thought how silly I had been.

'What did you think it was?' David asked, looking at me suspiciously.

'Oh, nothing,' I said, covering up. 'It's just that I thought it looked an old sort of car. I don't think I've ever seen one like that before.'

'They made scores of those Daimlers just after the war,'

said the clever lad. 'Mostly for weddings and funerals, of course.'

I thought: 'I mustn't let my imagination run away with me. How foolish can you get?'

'We wasted the run, anyway,' I said out loud.

'Yes. Mr Milner's waiting to meet the wedding party. Look.'

'Shall we go and have another look at the grave?' I suggested. 'Perhaps we can get the vicar between weddings.'

I stole a look at our possible benefactor. He seemed reassuring; an oldish, bespectacled man, with tousled hair ruffled by the slight breeze. Of course, he couldn't recognise us at the distance we were, and anyhow he had the weddings to bother him. He had a very courteous manner, perhaps like David in old age, I thought.

I had wanted to see the grave in daylight. I had an almost spooky feeling that the strange extra words would disappear in November daylight. I also wanted to check all round the grave to see if there was any other clue. I felt a bit reticent about my enthusiasm, though, till I found how keen David was. He charged off up the churchyard at a fine speed, much too fast for my lungs, which began to gasp again with discomfort.

'Wait,' I puffed out.

'Sorry,' he said, and immediately slowed down to a walk. Not a lot of people would do that for you, even girls. As for boys, they'd go all the faster.

We reached the grave, which was just as we'd seen it on Thursday night. *Innocent of all harm* was still engraved on it, very much clearer now that it was daylight.

'It doesn't look like a fake,' said David.

'But what a thing to put on! And how did we miss it the first time? I still can't figure that out.' I bent down to trace the writing with my finger, sliding my nail along the incised letters.

'The writing is a bit different, though, David,' pointed out. 'We thought so on Thursday.'

'It's properly cut in. It must have been done the same time,' I said.

A loud shout through the trees and bushes startled us both. I stepped back guiltily. It is funny how one can feel guilt even though there is nothing wrong at all. The verger came in sight, pushing a wheelbarrow. He was still dressed in the black gown he had used to welcome the wedding party into the church. Some people might have found the contrast between the gown and the wheelbarrow funny, but I was scared, a bit. David wasn't though.

'Good morning, Mr Cutler,' he exclaimed cheerfully.

'Oh! It's yo. I was a-wonderin' who'd be monkeyin' round them graves. Yo'n sid them on the far side, knocked over, I suppose? Last Thursday night, that was. Some o' the lads off'n the state come up and 'ad a beano, I reckon.'

'Teresa and I were only looking.'

'Ar. But I got enough to do to keep all this place tidy without kids, and old 'uns too, as ought to know better, bostin' up the graves.'

I didn't think this sounded very friendly, but David seemed not to mind.

'You see, this grave's got a very strange phrase on it. Have you ever noticed it, Mr Cutler?'

'Come 'ere. Let's 'ave a look.' Mr Cutler stepped on to the grave and bent down to read the writing, his black gown flapping round him.

'Ar,' he said, considering. 'Mind, I seem to think some o' these was covered in moss once. I believe they were. But I cor tell yer what that means, "Innocent of all 'arm". What 'arm could 'er do, the young wench?'

'We don't know. As a matter of fact, we've come to call on Mr Milner this morning specially to see if we can find any more out about her.'

' 'E'll be busy till half-eleven, yo know, Mr Milner will. There's another weddin' after this'n. But I'm afraid yo'll 'ave t'excuse me. I cor stand 'ere a-cantin' on. Got to get this wheelbarrow dumped and get back to the vestry for the signin'.'

'We'll take the load up for you,' David offered.

The verger thanked us and away he plodded, still odd in his ceremonial clothing. We took turns to push the creaky and lumbering old barrow up to the far end of the grave-yard, where there was an enormous heap of rubbish for burning. Pushing the barrow was almost worse than com-ing up the village street, and we were just as puffed at the end.

I hoisted myself on to the churchyard wall and sat down while David patiently juggled the barrow into position for tipping the rubbish.

'Come and sit up here a bit,' I called down, when he'd finished the job. 'It's lovely and peaceful up here.'

From the top of the wall you can see for miles, right over to the blue-green hills. And it was peaceful too, with nothing but the sound of the robin's disembodied autumn song.

'OK,' David answered. 'We've got about half an hour to wait before we can get in the vestry. It took us longer to get up the hill than I thought.'

He scrabbled on to the wall and sat a few feet off, gazing curiously at me.

'Teresa, you did sound excited about that car. What did you think you'd seen?'

I changed the subject, embarrassed. 'Funny up in the graveyard, isn't it?' I said. 'All these dead people around. I don't wonder folk find graveyards spooky.'

'How do you mean?'

'Well. Under the grave where we were standing, if we'd dug down we could find Abigail's bones, couldn't we? The bones of an almost full-grown female. But nothing to say it was her, not really. No actual person any more, just a skeleton.'

'Yes.'

'Well, then. Churchy people say folk go on after they're dead, don't they? I know they do, and they seem to believe it. I mean, Mom and Dad go to the Wesleyan, and they say so. I don't think they're just kidding me because I'm only a child.'

'Mr Milner says so too.'

That reminded me that David came to this church on Sundays, and belonged here. To me this seemed a queer thing to do. Surely he was too old for churches?

'I tell you what,' I said intensely. 'I don't believe a word of it. Not one word. I just don't think there are super-natural things, not really, any more than Father Christmas.'

My passionate speech must have surprised him, because he moved a little further off. I was really a bit scared of getting into an argument on this topic. My anti-religious feelings were a bit new, and slightly private. But I couldn't stop now; I was launched.

'For instance: would God let innocent people die? And they do, without doing anyone any harm at all. You've only got to look at the telly to see that. I don't think there's a God, truly I don't.'

'Well,' the boy replied, a little bit coolly, 'I'm being confirmed. Next year it is, so I don't agree with you.'

'I'm not arguing, David. You can think what you like. It's just that I care about good people dying, but God never does anything. So there isn't a God.'

'But going back to what you said before,' he went on. 'I agree it is a bit spooky up here. What was that about dead people?'

'I only wanted to know what you think about them. I mean, is that all there is of them, just bones?'

'Look, Teresa. You won't believe what I say if I do tell you. You've already laughed at me for coming here on Sundays.' He looked earnest, with his eyes aglow.

'I didn't mean to laugh, really I didn't. I said you could think what you like. Don't let's fall out over it.'

'Sorry,' he said. 'I'm not really touchy. But Mr Milner has ways of telling you about dying and about dead people. I've listened to him carefully, and I must say I think he could be right. I don't believe this "dead and done for" idea, anyhow.'

I had a lot of mixed up feelings about this chat. It was very cosy, sitting on that high wall in our own world, and I was warm inside with the friendliness of talking on so serious a subject. But also I was a bit shivery with nerves, just because it was so important. It seemed so strange to be sitting in a churchyard talking about death all surrounded by the dead, and David suggesting that in some way they might not be. I had more than half a mind to accept his idea so far as dying went. But I knew I was determined not to believe in any God, because I knew a good God could have managed things better than letting babies starve in India.

I ventured another point. 'What about ghosts? Do you think they exist?'

'I don't know. Ghosts aren't part of religion. But you could class both as "the supernatural".'

'I don't think there's any supernatural,' I said firmly.

'All right. But the thing I think is, that life's more complicated than people suppose. I know a lot of folk think science has unproved things, but really it hasn't proved or unproved anything at all. There's lots of things I mean to find out, myself.'

'Oh, David. You are serious. You really care about it.'

I remember staring closely at him, seeing his frowning forehead and puzzling, thoughtful eyes. I could see that for him, logic would be all important. Whereas with me, it is feelings that count.

The next minute he slid off the wall—yes, slid right off. I think that churchyard must have some queer effect on him; that was twice he'd fallen over in one week. This time, he'd scrazed his hand on a jagged stone, and I mopped it up for him with a dirty handkerchief he produced from his pocket. I don't suppose it could have done any good. It's a wonder he didn't get gangrene or something. In the end the blood stopped oozing through the handkerchief on to my fingers, and I thought he'd survive. But to have his blood on my fingers was strange; it made me feel almost sick at first, then it became mysterious, as if it united us.

'You'll live now,' I pronounced.

'We'll have to hurry back,' he said. 'That wedding should be over by now. I make it just coming up to five and twenty past.'

4
A Terrible Accident

At the church door the photographers were swarming, and people were shivering because they hadn't known what to wear for this November wedding and had thought of looks before comfort. Auntie this and cousin that were having a quiet giggle, but the bride and groom were looking a bit scared. That's odd when I think of it, but perhaps it is a bit scaring to promise something 'till death us do part'. David knew the back way to the vestry, and we were lucky because Mr Milner was just coming down the back steps. He greeted us with a cheery smile.

'I wondered where you'd got to. We'll have to be quick. Saturday's a busy day in this trade. And who's this?'

'Teresa Willetts,' I answered, looking at the doorstep. Somehow I felt upset and embarrassed appearing at this vicar's church with David. Perhaps it was because of what I'd said on the wall, or it could have been something else.

Then we all went into the vestry, and I saw a dark table, faded photographs on the white walls, a high window and a dark green painted iron safe. I had never seen such a large one before. It had the names of the churchwardens for the year 1812 on it and creaked open in an impressive way when the vicar turned the key in the lock. A musty volume, rather large, came out in his hands. The edges of all the pages were charred and brittle, so that as he turned them bits crumbled off however careful he was; how horrifying that historical documents should crumble away like this!

He told us, as I already knew, that the church had been burnt to the ground in a terrible fire just before the First World War. Only because of the firemen's tremendous courage in dragging out the document chest could we read anything about Abigail's burial.

At last we reached the right page, and by the yellow glow of the gas light which lit the vestry we read the entry for December 14th 1860, four days after her death. It gave no age, no reason for the girl's death, no clue: only her name, and her father's name, Henry Parkes, and their place of residence, 'Gosty Hill', a windswept crest overlooking the tube works on one side, a dark canal on the other, and fading away into other hills by Waterfall Lane. The book lay on the table, the page stayed open.

'What's the interest in this girl?' asked Mr Milner. 'A school project, is it?'

'Not exactly,' David answered. 'We just got interested after we'd copied the gravestone. She just seemed an interesting kind of person.'

I didn't feel satisfied with that answer. He hadn't mentioned the 'Innocent of all harm' on the grave, which I thought was the reason I was so keen. Or was there some other reason, I vaguely wondered. Why should we both be so ready to follow up this girl's story? And was David's reason the same as mine?

'You might find out more from the death certificate,' Mr Milner said. 'You'd get that from Somerset House in London if you wrote to them. You'd have to pay, about thirty or forty pence, I think. It'd tell you the cause of death, and you'd have the name of a witness. Of course, if she died suddenly there'd be an inquest. You could try the *Birmingham Gazette* and see if there's anything in.'

'I will write to Somerset House; that's a good idea,' David replied. 'Perhaps you could tell me what to write . . .'

If they were going to be boring and businesslike, I had

my own thoughts to turn to. Besides, I felt a bit resentful at the bond of 'churchiness' they had between them, and even a bit scared in case David would tell Mr Milner what I'd said on the churchyard wall. If he did, I'd never speak to him again. To get away from them both, I looked at the parish register on the old brown table. The writing was antique, probably copperplate, but quite readable. *Abigail Parkes*, it said. But what was this, by the side of the entry? A cross in faded ink which I hadn't noticed before, and a spidery ink line running from the cross to the foot of the page. The lad and the vicar were well away in churchy talk by now, and I bent close over the page in the book. My maddening shadow came between the page and the gas light.

'Oh, cuss it,' I said beneath my breath.

Then I held the book carefully up to the light, and read these words in charred mottly brown: *She died in the canal near Wright's Bridge on December 10th, an excessively dark and windy night. It was a terrible accident.*

As I read those words, I knew I should always remember them, especially the last sentence. Whatever happened later, the writing would stay clearly printed on my mind. And so it has proved to be.

'Ah, well,' said the vicar, suddenly. 'It seems I can't be much help to you.'

Little did he know he was just going to be a big hindrance. He swept up the register to put it back in the safe.

'Just a minute!' I shrieked, meaning to show my great discovery. The vicar dropped the book in surprise. The page slipped out and the charred edge crumbled on impact with the floor. It was, indeed, a terrible accident to our evidence, for when we picked up the page, the bottom part, about a quarter of an inch, was gone—dust to dust and ashes to ashes.

'What is it?' asked the vicar, red-faced and rather alarmed.

'Nothing,' I sadly said, shaking my head. 'Nothing really. It must have been my imagination.'

And though I told David about it afterwards, I couldn't prove it had really been there. But the words 'It was a terrible accident' rang in my head, and made me do what I did afterwards.

That night I had a bath by order of Mom. She was right enough, really, because dirt off the graveyard and dirt off the charred bits of register was grimed into me. But even in those days, I didn't like bathrooms, and I don't like them now. I can't make people understand this. The warmth of the water is all right, I suppose. But our bathroom is eerie; it has odd little echoes in it, and makes little noises sound quite loud. You can peer up at the ceiling and not see it for steam, and the window catch rattles in the wind. The lovely bright sitting-room is in another world. Odd, eerie thoughts come to me in the bathroom.

I was thinking about my day and two important people, David Ray and Abigail Parkes. David puzzled me a good deal. However I thought about him, I could make nothing romantic of him. Sometimes he seemed babyish, with his floppy fawn scarf and his voice like a glede under a door. I shuddered at the thought of his dirty school blazer and sighed forlornly for something else. On the other hand, he was polite, and his politeness seemed to mean something, as if he really cared about people, not just me of course but everyone. He seemed to know so much, and I envied him this gift.

The frothy soap bubbled round my neck. I was in a proper dream; I seemed to sense some mystery in every soap bubble, if only I could discover what it meant. The taps at the other end of the bath barely showed through the steam, and I felt as if I was looking through the wrong end of a telescope at them. They were just like people, I thought, tantalisingly near, yet so far away. One was David, the other Abigail. I shouldn't ever get to know much about those two, yet somehow I felt I'd like to *be* them, either or both.

I seemed to know Abigail better than David. How odd that she met her end in the canal, just a few hundred yards from our house, on a stormy December night! I pictured her as very beautiful, with eyes my own dark blue like the ones that can stare soulfully back at me from the mirror. Of course, I don't mean I'm beautiful, or ever will be. Val is only too right when she tells me this. As for Abigail, water had quenched her beauty and her life, by some terrible accident. I felt the water round myself, and wondered what it would be like if I could never get out. 'I can get out now, this minute,' I thought. 'My head's above water. My lungs can breathe air. This bath is only playing with water. But she couldn't get out. I suppose she tried, if it wasn't suicide. But she drowned; she was immersed and the softly eddying liquid flowed over her. She felt it getting into her lungs, her eyes, her ears, everywhere. Looking down from the surface, you'd only be able to see great rings, then smaller disturbances, then finally silence, stillness.'

I got very miserable at the thought of the beautiful girl and her wasted life. But I got determined, too; certain that I should find out everything about her. I could feel her distant spirit fluttering, beseeching me to understand her and believe in her innocence, as the gravestone told me.

Jean clattered into the room, looking splendid. She, like the Abigail of my dreams, has dark blue eyes, and her hair is sleek blonde when she's brushed it. She must have been solidly brushing away in our room for half an hour.

'Oh, gosh, Tess! Are you still here? Whatever are you

doing? You'll wash away to nothing if you don't come out soon!'

'You're off with Steve tonight, I suppose,' I said, not answering her.

'I'm supposed to be at the Plaza now, this minute. And I do believe you've had all the hot water!'

Truly, I do envy Jean. It must be really marvellous to be grown up enough to have freedom, but not old enough to have too much responsibility. Then, as well, Jean is as beautiful as I thought Abigail might be, instead of freckled and foolish like me, a betwixt and between creature. Honestly, at my age you don't count either as a child or as a real person: to be thirteen and a half is really sickening!

5
The Inquest Report

I've never been to a real inquest. I should think it'd be
boring. But I didn't mind too much looking up Abigail's
inquest, as David and I did the Wednesday afterwards in
our reference library.

Our reference library is a huge modern building with
absolutely thousands of books everywhere, storing enormous wisdom in them. Swarms of students in all kinds of
strange gear are drinking in the wisdom, or else chewing
the ends of their pencils, or talking very quietly, or dreaming up at the roof. There are also some older people, very
serious and grey-haired, frowning at the talking students.
Every quarter of an hour a booming clock reminds you of
the time, and the quarters go so fast you get startled by the
speed of it. Time seems to shrivel up to nothing.

The booming clock, usually called 'Big Brum', was
frightening the pigeons with its chime when we got off the
red bus beneath it. The dusky November evening was
closing in. Golden street lights made the hurrying people
seem ghostly, but I like the centre of Birmingham at that
time. Below, everyone is rushing to catch their buses,
yellow and blue or bright red. They all clutch newspapers
in their grimy hands, intent on home and a rest. Over their
heads wheel as many starlings, chattering and jabbering so
loud that they drown the traffic sounds. And like the people,
they are looking for a rest. You can see them shuffling on
to the ledges of the buildings, pushing and jostling for a
place; then if there's no room a group will take to the air

again and rove round the square to find another windowsill. As far as you can look into the sky, there are busy flocks flying in from remote parts of the Midlands. Not one of them is still: like the people below they rush and bustle and flap, full of nervous energy.

But David and I were soon immersed in another world. The faded old newspapers, bound in an immense leather cover, were dreadfully heavy. It took the two of us to stagger across to a study table with them. The boy student opposite looked up sourly as we hoisted the huge volume up: he didn't like the idea of kids interrupting his hard work. Even opening the file and turning the pages was difficult; such a musty brown they were, I was afraid they would go the way of the parish register page. Never mind, we turned them somehow, and found December 1860.

SUICIDE ATTEMPT SUCCEEDS.
RESCUERS FOILED BY RAINY NIGHT

That was the headline of the short report on Abigail's death.

Last night in heavy rain a girl, believed to be about seventeen, ran into the canal at Old Hill. Mr Wright, of the Sportsman Inn, tried unsuccessfully to drag her out, and he was soon joined by others, including Mr David Caddick, a collier, of Gosty Hill. Mr Caddick dived into the canal despite the dreadful downpour and searched for some considerable time for the body. It being found in a water-logged and foul condition some hours later, the rescuing party had the mournful task of carrying it to the Sportsman, awaiting identification. There is unfortunately little doubt that suicide was intended. The girl had been seen wandering in the area for some days in low spirits.

When we looked at the next day's paper we read:

IDENTIFICATION OF OLD HILL SUICIDE.
RESPECTED MINE-OWNER'S DAUGHTER DROWNED

The identity of the young lady drowned in the canal at Old Hill has now been discovered. She is Miss Abigail Parkes, daughter of

Mr Henry Parkes, a local coal proprietor. It is feared she committed suicide, having been in very poor spirits the last week as the members of the household have stated. So stormy was the night that no one heard her fall until Mr Wright went out to look at the lanterns. Mrs Parkes, the dead girl's mother, is confined to her room with the shock of the discovery. The coroner will sit on the body at West Bromwich court at a time to be arranged.

Everything now depended on the inquest itself. It was with jittery fingers that we turned the fragile pages until we found the reports of the coroner's court. At the time, we made notes, taking it in turns, with a break in the middle for orange squash in the café. But I've written it here in modern language, without leaving anything out, or putting anything in that wasn't in the original.

The first thing the coroner did was to call in the people who discovered the body, Mr Wright of the Sportsman and others. This pub of Mr Wright's was just over the canal bridge where the road leads down from Gosty Hill to Old Hill. It's still there now, just the same. I sensed Mr Wright was a sober witness, calm, properly Victorian. He was a bit above the colliers and sinkers, brickmakers and labourers who came to his pub to drink.

It must have been a wretched stormy night. Darkness fell early, and the pelting rain combined with a shrill wind to create a pandemonium in which branches snapped off trees and slates hurtled from roofs. There weren't many customers hardy enough to brave the weather for their pint of ale that night. Mr Wright had seen Abigail run past, her clothes sodden and her hair blown out, wet as it was, by the violent gale. He had watched her stop, in all that rain, in the middle of the hump-backed bridge over the canal. It seems he heard no shout, or anything like that, but when he looked out a minute or two later, worried about the girl, he saw a swirl in the water of the canal and ran full tilt to the towpath side across the bridge.

When he got there, breathless, he was joined by some other men, including his servant Elijah, a young collier called Caddick—who turned out to be important—and an elderly miner, Zachariah Oakley. They caught hold of branches and sticks to probe the canal, shouted to the girl to show where she was, waved their guttering and feeble lanterns over the canal's gloomy waters, stamped along the bank and through the reeds at the edge. More lanterns were called for, and Mr Wright ran like the wind to Old Hill town to find them. Because of this, he missed the moment when the body was found.

David Caddick actually found it, and brought it out of the canal. The coroner called him next. He had been whistling in the dark as he came down the hill from the Black Bank pit to keep his spirits up. Why should he need to keep his spirits up? The coroner, without realising it, had stumbled on a family skeleton. As the questions went on, it was revealed that between David Caddick the rough collier and Miss Parkes the proprietor's daughter, there had been an 'association' which had provoked her father to wild rage. He had discovered them twice, talking together at the end of the drive to the house. He had flicked his horsewhip round the collier's neck in a cruel Victorian way, threatening to dismiss him from his job as butty collier.

'And I wish he had dismissed me, sir. I was working at that time at Fiery Holes mine, not far from Black Bank, where I work now.' (At the time I couldn't get the drift of this, and it was a long time before I understood.)

As the man spoke, a violent interruption shocked the court. A pale middle-aged woman stood up in the hall and shook her fist at the witness.

'It's you that caused my daughter's death,' she screamed. 'Only for you she'd still be alive.'

The newspaper reporter must have enjoyed Mrs Parkes' sensation, but the collier lad did not. He hid his face in his hands for shame and sorrow. There were more questions to ask him yet.

'How did you find her, in the end?' the coroner demanded.

'I saw nothing for it, sir, but to get into the canal and swim. I much doubted she could still be alive, but I had my hopes and I knew there was not a second to be lost. I took off my jacket and jumped in to comb the canal, swimming from side to side, testing the weeds, the reed beds and the overhanging trees to feel whether her clothes had caught in them. Of course, there was almost no light from the lanterns, which kept blowing out with the wind's force.

'I gradually moved down from the bridge towards the bend in the canal, scraping against the side of boats moored by the towpath, which I couldn't see in the dark. It was a ghastly task, you'll readily understand, feeling for a person's body among the flotsam in the water, and knowing the body might be dead and sunk to the bottom. But it had to be done: there was a small chance that she might be alive.

'I found her tangled in the rushes as I'd thought, not more than ten yards from the bridge. I cannot tell the detail, sir, and hope one day to forget. Together we dragged her out and laid her on the bank, just as Mr Wright came back with new lights and the doctor. But of course, all life had left her, and her spirit had passed over to her Maker. May he have mercy on her. Now, I must really beg your pardon, sir, and pray you to dismiss me.'

A deep sigh escaped me as I read that, and David looked at me in concern. Still, we now knew how the body was found. But was there any witness to Abigail's leap from the bridge? Zachariah Oakley, an ageing collier who had worked under Caddick, seemed to know the most about this. He spoke, I am sure, in a broad local dialect. He must have been full of sorrow, and nervous too to find himself in court. But he spoke truly, and his evidence was important, more so than anyone seemed to notice.

'It was a very stormy night, sir, as I was a-comin' down past Slack Hillock. 'Twas black as black, and even an old miner as con see in the dark cor see everything. It's a lonely track too, and yo' do' meet a dog down there most nights. This time, though, I could hear runnin' feet over the sound of the wind. I dain't have no idea who was a-runnin' nor where from. I couldn't see ne'er a thing against I come in sight of Wright's public, on the fur bank of the cut. Then by the light of the lanterns at the front of the house I sid this wench, sir, a-runnin' off'n the fordrove on to the bridge.

'Well, 'er come to the midpoint and stopped, a-lookin' down into the water. I was near the bridge by this, and 'eard 'er cry out sudden. It crossed me mind to goo and ask if there was summat I could do for 'er. But I'd likely have scared 'er. So I goes on me way, sorry for 'er trouble.'

'No splash?' asked the coroner.

'Well, sir. I was some yards along the towpath afore I looked back. I sid th' outline of the wench a-walkin' off'n the bridge then. I dain't stop, though. I went on along the towpath. A minute after, I looked again. 'Er'd gone, clean gone. This was when they come a-runnin' from the 'ouse, sir, Mr Wright and Elijah Round. They called me back, and we searched the bank. David Caddick come along, and jumped in the water, and still we all searched and peered in the rain and keen wind for above an hour. They found 'er at last, in the cut, as yo' knowen.'

Whatever made Abigail do it? To run out into the stormy dark, to jump into the blackness of the cut, to be so despairing and so destructive . . . Why did she do it?

'She was worse than usual that night, sir,' said the next witness. 'She'd peer out of the window, harkening to the rain. She'd wander to the fireplace, and hold on to the mantel for support. She'd study her reflection in the brass ornaments and fiddle with the ring on her finger. While I was scouring the floor, she was traipsing all round me, never still a minute.'

The kitchen maid's tiny voice could hardly be heard in the courtroom, and the coroner told her to speak up. In those days the kitchens were scrubbed by girls no older than our first-formers. Their tasks were endless: they lit fires, set tables, fetched and carried all the time. Susanna Caddick was one of these.

'Her state of mind, please, girl?' asked the coroner.

'She would walk about all day, always restless the whole week, she was. Then she'd come in from wandering round the tump and over the pit banks and trail dirt over the quarries in the passage and kitchen. She was for ever running her fingers through her hair . . .' ('Speak up!') 'Through her hair, sir; and doing and undoing her buttons.'

'And are you the sister of Caddick, the witness who dragged the body from the canal?'

'Yes, sir.'

'Did you know of the association between them?'

'I couldn't say at all, sir. Mr Parkes the master had given me orders that David must not come to see me any more. He was never meant to, but he did in times gone by. The master said it was a liberty he couldn't abide. That's all I know.'

'But why was Miss Parkes in the kitchen that evening?'

(Here the witness dropped her voice again) 'She seemed to trust me . . .'

'The court cannot hear you,' thundered the coroner.

'She seemed to trust me, sir. She talked to me at times, and liked to be with me.'

'You? A domestic? Why ever should she? Because you were a link with your brother?'

'Oh, I can't say, sir. It was a bad week that week. It was a fearful time for all. We were all distressed at the mine disaster, and sick with fear.'

But it was no use. The coroner couldn't understand what the girl was trying to say, and he couldn't believe Abigail had chosen Susanna Caddick for company. He puzzled and probed with his questions till she seemed to lose her voice. Yet he never asked the question I felt like asking, about the mine disaster she'd mentioned. In the end he gave up and dismissed the timid servant. Then he called Henry Parkes.

Abigail's father was bluff and dignified on the surface, but I thought his heartiness hid a wild sorrow, not very different from his wife's.

'When did you find out about the connection between your daughter and Caddick?' asked the coroner.

'I could not agree that it reached a point where I should call it a connection.'

'The association, then.'

'Acquaintance, I will allow.'

'When did you know of their acquaintance?'

'I saw Caddick talking to my daughter on two occasions at the end of the carriage drive. I broke up their meeting at once, and they did not meet again. I forbade her to go out or see him.'

'Do you think, Mr Parkes, that she could have killed herself because you had forbidden her to see Caddick?'

'She did not kill herself. She must have slipped in from the slimy towpath. She could not kill herself. It was impossible to her, such an action.' And Mr Parkes would not be moved from his belief, even though it was so different from his wife's outburst, 'It's you that caused my daughter's death.'

In the end the wife's theory was believed. The coroner must have decided there was some close friendship between Abigail and David Caddick which had been broken, after which the girl had drowned herself in the canal that

December night. He brought in a suicide verdict, and so the newspaper report closed.

'Funny, finding a David in the story,' I said, as we grappled with the newspaper file and took it back to the librarian.

'Well, it wasn't me, for sure,' said David Ray, blinking behind his glasses as he tried to focus on the distance after reading.

'I never said it was. Perhaps it was your great-grand-father.'

'It wouldn't be actually,' he answered, taking me seriously. 'I was born in Cheshire, in fact.'

'No one could tell, to hear you talk.'

'Near Manchester, at Sale.'

'Oh. I always imagine everyone at our school has ancestors going back to Methusalah in our town. They mostly seem to. I mean, the only one of our family that doesn't live round here is my Nanny at Weston. And she used to live at Blackheath.'

'Well, you can have Blackheath as far as I'm concerned. Though I suppose I'm used to it.'

By this time we were at the doors, shivering in the cold November air, then walking thoughtfully by the Town Hall to the bus stop. Round about us, high on the ledges, the starlings shuffled and squawked in restless sleep, rowed up there in their thousands. It made me think of a poem called 'Flannan Isle' which we did at school. In it 'three black ugly birds' sat brooding over a scene where three lighthouse keepers had disappeared. Some of us thought the birds might have been the men's souls, and I wondered if the starlings were the souls of thousands of dead Midlanders. But no, it really was a stupid idea, to think that people could turn into starlings.

It did remind me, though, of what I'd said to David about people going back to Methuselah round our way. You've only got to look in the churchyard to see how the names repeat for fifty, a hundred, two hundred years. My grandad Willetts made chain, and I know for a fact that his grandad made chain too, and had the same name, Joseph Willetts. And it's only ten minutes' walk from our house to where they both worked, so I'd know my great-grandad if I met him, I would certainly. And I don't really think he'd look like a starling, perched on the Town Hall. Not even as much as we did, David and me, sitting up on the top deck of the bus as we chattered about the evening's work, while my heart warmed to the characters involved in the inquest, sad Abigail, brave David and timid, kind Susanna—even tough and sorrowing Henry Parkes.

6
The Old Mine Shaft

Steve, Jean's boyfriend, opened the door to me when I got home.

'You've missed the fun, young Teresa,' he said. He is very teasing sometimes, and I can't get back at him because he's very clever and going to be a teacher.

'Let's get my coat off,' I answered. 'Then you can tell me what fun.'

'Your dad didn't think it was funny though.'

'Oh, shut up, and don't keep talking in riddles.'

I walked in and hung my coat up on the wall, not far from the sampler. Steve disappeared into the front room where I heard him tell Jean it was me come home.

'D'you want anything to eat, our Teresa?' she called through the open door. 'Bit late, aren't you?'

'It's only just gone nine,' I answered with dignity.

'You've been in the wicked city, though.'

'Only in the reference library; that's no den of vice!'

'That I wouldn't know.' She hovered round the door as she spoke. 'Well, do you want any supper? There's a bun on the kitchen table.'

'Thanks,' I said, nodding to the sampler, collecting the bun, and seating myself in the front room with the starry-eyed pair.

'What's the fun about?' I enquired through a mouthful of bun. 'The house is still standing, anyway, I notice.'

'It might not have been,' Steve answered. 'It's only luck. Your dad's cabbages have gone for a Burton anyway.'

I put the bun down and stared at him with my mouth open.

'Little men from middle earth came up this afternoon,' he went on. 'They've had the army here, M.I.5, goodness knows who!'

'Oh, Steve, tell her properly,' Jean cut in.

'Well, the police and the fire-brigade anyway,' Steve corrected himself.

For a minute I considered where Mom and Dad were. They'd said they were going down to choir practice as usual, but had they been rushed off in an ambulance? I must have begun to look a bit nervous, because Steve rapidly changed the tone of his voice and said seriously,

'No, honestly, Tess. The cabbages are gone, but everything else is all right and your mom and dad are down the Wesleyan. About half past ten this morning there was a terrible rumble and your mom rushed out into the fold just in time to see a slanty line come all across the vegetable plot, and a hole in the middle as big as an outhouse.'

'The police came, and the fire brigade,' Jean explained. 'They were here when I got in from work. A great big fire engine right across the gate. Didn't half make Mr Parkes cross, him with his beautiful Jaguar which he couldn't get in his garage.'

'But what is it? Is it safe? Are we safe?' I queried. 'What do we want the fire-brigade for?'

'They checked the house was safe,' Steve answered. 'It's lucky your garden's so long. It's an old pit shaft, subsided. It's always happening, you know. A few years ago there was one at Brickhouse that was in all the papers. Some folk say half the new houses in the Midlands are on old mine shafts.'

'They use concrete rafts, though, don't they?' Jean suggested.

'Well, they do for the pits they know about. But their

maps only go back so far, and if it didn't exist in 1900, it didn't exist at all, they think.'

'And really a good many mines had been abandoned by then,' I went on, seeing his point.

'Yes. There were all sorts of reasons why they gave them up. An underground fire, for instance. That would make the mine impossible to work, so they'd give it up. I think there's still a notice about fires underground at Netherton churchyard, or has been till recently. Or else the old miners came to a fault in the ground; and they never bothered to fill the old shafts in when they abandoned them.'

'So Dad's cabbages were resting on a few feet of soil,' I summarised. 'And we're all bloomin' lucky he never fell in. It jolly well makes you think.'

I picked up the bun and bit it viciously. To think that was all the old miners cared for anyone that might come after! To think people would build houses all over the derelict pits! To think our dad might have broken his neck while quietly digging his cabbage patch one Saturday morning, for all his fifty or so performances in the 'Hallelujah Chorus'!

A bit later on I excused myself and went out into the moonshiny garden to see if there was anything to see. I dursn't walk far up the path, but from a vantage point near the cold frame I spotted chaos ahead instead of the vegetable patch. Some of the cabbages seemed to have sunk in the ground, while others lay with their roots exposed. We should be having early spring cabbage for weeks from now on!

I stared into the dark. The inquest scene was still running through my mind; and as I stood there I realised that Fiery Holes mine, where David Caddick had worked before he moved to Black Bank, must be close by our house. It could be that our cabbages had collapsed into the very mine I had just read about. The more I stood and looked, the surer I became. Suddenly I heard the front door chimes ring, and ran in to answer.

An aged but cheerful voice greeted me when I opened the door: 'Hullo, my wench. Is yer dad in?'

'No, Mr Downing. He's still down the Wesleyan. Better come in,' I answered.

'Thank you, m'dear,' he said, stepping into the hall. He took off his cap and muffler, revealing hair as silver as the moonlight.

'Put them on the stair post,' I said.

'Ta, love.' The old man shuffled over to the stairs and hung up his cap and scarf.

'It's about the mine shaft,' he went on. 'I thought I'd best drap in and tell yer dad all I know on it. 'Cos I'll bet 'e's mithered, is 'e?'

'I don't think he'll be long,' I told him. 'Best come in the front room a bit. Jean's in with Stephen, her boyfriend.'

I ushered the little white-haired man in and he took a seat on the settee. Steve and Jean greeted him affably. It turned out he knew Steve's parents, uncles, cousins and everyone else in Steve's family.

'But I a'a sid thee since thee wast a babby,' he finished.

'Well, how's that then?' Steve asked, dropping into a thick dialect in talking to this old man. ' 'Cos I was reared at Great Bridge, 'tother side Dudley Port. I dai' know as I'd any origins this way.'

'Ar. 'Twas in Dudley market I sid thee, in a little pram. Eighteen 'ear or more agone. I've got the right chap, though, I know.'

This grown-up gossip was getting boring. It is just marvellous how, round our way, folk can't rest until they've traced your pedigree for you, and proved they knew your great-grandfather. But I wanted to know about the mine.

'What were you going to tell Dad about the shaft?' I asked.

'Oh, ar. A real ode 'un that shaft is. 'Twor never used when I wun a lad, but we knowed wheer it was. They'd 'a thraped we to dyeath if we'd 'a played up that part o' the field. Fiery Holes, that was. Finished, it did, after a fire killed me grandfaeyther and some others in it. O' course, they ne'er filled it in, they wun that near with they money. 'Ears and 'ears afore I was born, it was, but me dad knowed all about it. I doubt as yer dad won't get no compensation money. The family as owned these 'ere pits died out 'ears agone. I cor rightly say who'd be the heir to them if there was any. They'm dyead and gone, long since.'

I thought of Henry Parkes, and wondered if he'd had any other children besides Abigail.

Then I heard the front door creak, and decided to scram quickly. I'd only been allowed to go into Birmingham after school on the strict understanding I wasn't late in bed. But here it was past ten o'clock, and me not so much as upstairs.

'Goodnight, Mom; Goodnight, Dad,' I shouted over my shoulder as they walked into the hall. 'I'm glad the cabbages were the only thing that fell into the hole, I really am.'

I never stopped to discuss, though. There are times when a tired retreat to bed is a jolly useful stopper on inquisitive lips. But . . . just fancy! Fiery Holes was in our garden!

7
'I Fell Into a Dream'

In a way, the mystery of Abigail Parkes was now cleared up. David Ray and I had read an actual account of the coroner's court in which her suicide had been proved. This explained why the funeral had been so small and poor, and why the clergyman had seemed so unhappy when he buried her. It explained the mingy grave inscription (except for the 'Innocent of all harm') and the early age of death.

The only thing was, I just didn't believe it. As I pithered about in the bedroom that night, after leaving my parents in such a hurry, I worked away on Abigail's character, trying to picture why she had died. Even the court evidence didn't actually prove suicide, as far as I could see. What was supposed to be the motive, that her friendship with David Caddick had been broken off, didn't seem enough to make anyone do such a thing.

Agreed, I could recall a ballad, 'Barbara Allen', in which a man pines away because his sweetheart 'just doesn't want to know'. It always seemed a most fearful ballad when we did it in the junior school. It seemed to mean it might be possible to die for love, and that made love a dangerous thing. But then, that was a ballad, Abigail was real. I decided to try to work out a bit about her life with David.

I could imagine Abigail meeting him for the first time. It was one day when he came to visit his sister, I decided. I took an empty school notebook to bed with me, switched on the reading lamp, and began to write about it. For this too, if the parents got to know, I should 'cop out'.

One dark Sunday—I began—Abigail Parkes heard the sound of conversation in the kitchen of the rambling house where she lived. She could hear a man's voice talking to Susanna, the serving girl, who was supposed to be washing and cleaning after supper. Abigail felt guilty loitering in the passage outside, but she knew this man should not be here without her father's knowledge. Susanna shouldn't have visitors on Sunday night, should she? Despite the green baize door the words of their conversation were almost audible. The tones were mellow and strong, the warm local speech rising and falling, the girl's laughter frothing out at times amid the sound of water swilling crockery.

'No. I won't tell father,' Abigail said to herself. 'But I must just know who the man is.'

She took several silent steps to the door. After all, Susanna was a friend almost as much as a servant to her. She couldn't mind if Abigail visited the kitchen tonight, for this was what she often did in the evening. Suddenly a crock crashed to the floor behind the baize door. Impulsively Abigail rushed to the door and opened it, hurling herself into the firelit room, where her entry caused a flurry of surprise. A fine china shepherdess had splintered into pieces across the red quarry tiles. Little Susanna's eyes widened with shock as she held the drying cloth, and the man looked up from the fireplace where he had been stirring the fire into a blaze.

'What are you doing, dropping my shepherd girl?' Abigail shouted. 'It was a careless thing to do. If they get to know, they'll stop your wages. And I can't stop them knowing! And what is this man doing, messing with our kitchen fire?'

The way Abigail talked surprised me, even as I wrote. I had been building up a picture of her as rather meek, yet here she was in my story brimming over with anger, wild with the servant, whom I'd thought of as her friend. Still, the words had almost written themselves: this was how she must have spoken.

I continued to write, a little apprehensively.

The maid knelt down—I went on—and picked up the broken crockery. She placed the ruins gently by the yellow sink, and turned her back in tears. Abigail stopped dead in her tracks, touched by the forlorn figure in the leaping firelight.

'Oh, Susanna, I didn't mean to be cross,' she said. 'I'm sure you couldn't help it. I'm sorry, I really am. Don't take any notice of me, I'm impulsive.'

But Susanna wouldn't be comforted. She continued to cry in a subdued and mournful way.

'Come on,' said Abigail. 'It's only a little statue. If it was a real person smashed like that, you'd need to cry. But it's not worth spoiling your evening for. Cheer up!'

The maid turned round, still heartbroken. The stranger watched with mingled surprise and embarrassment from the hearth, where the fire was by now burning greedily. There was no other light in the room for the three, only the radiant firelight by which the young man knelt.

'Oh, Miss. I'm sure I never meant it to happen. I never did, I swear. What a terrible accident! Oh, your lovely little statue, smashed in a second! I can't ever bring her back!'

'Well, Susanna. You were canting away to your friend.'

'Friend? Who? Oh, Miss. That's David, my brother, as works in the Fiery Holes pit for your dad. He hasn't got no right to be here, Miss, but he sometimes comes of a Sunday to help with the fire and tell me about the preaching. I've tried to stop him, but I can't make him keep away. Now, stand up, David, and pay your respects.'

The miner stood up . . . The miner stood up . . . It was no good. I couldn't keep my eyes awake, even though I felt very moved to write. I yawned and the biro dropped out of my hand on to the bedroom floor. I switched the light off and snuggled the pillow round me. Yet still I didn't feel as if I could let the matter rest. That reference library evening had been no good for me, together with the excitement of the vanishing cabbages! Before five minutes were over, I was surprised to find myself going on with the story, writing more vividly than before.

'Good evening, Miss,' said David. He looked not much older than Abigail, a little taller, with dark hair, rather long, and a clean-shaven face. His clothes were worn but proper, as was only right for a Sunday evening after chapel.

Susanna came into clear focus, now that the fire burnt so brightly. She was only about twelve, and was hopping about nervously near the sink, with the crocks at last dried and the pans stacked.

'Oh, Abigail, you did look bothered,' she said. 'You really did.'

'It was this voice in the kitchen I heard. I didn't know who it was. And then I heard the statue smash.'

'Well, David had nothing to do with it. He helps to mend things, not breaks them. But no one could mend her now, she's gone for good.'

'Anyway, I'm glad to see your brother, Susanna. He looks like you.'

Susanna sat on the window-seat, David stood with his back to the fire, and Abigail walked towards the window, though the bright reflection of the firelight prevented anything outside being seen.

'You were going to sing for me,' said the maid, looking keen, just like one of the first-formers at our school as she hunched her knees up to her chin on the window seat. She was thrilled and absorbed, just like I've seen David Ray when he spots some new thing, even in school work. While she watched and listened to his singing her eyes grew round, her face became serious, and her cheeks glowed against the stark black and white of her servant's dress.

This was what David Caddick sang:

As I went out in springtime to take the pleasant air,
I spied a fair young damsel down by a river clear.
She wept and she lamented, and bitterly she cried,
Saying 'My curse upon the cruel mine where Johnny Southern
   died.'

My love he was a collier lad and worked beneath the ground;
For modest mild demeanour his equal can't be found.
His teeth are white as ivory, his cheek a rosy red,
But alas, my handsome collier lies numbered with the dead.

Last night as I lay on my bed, I fell into a dream;
I dreamed a voice came to me, and called me by my name,
Saying 'Jeannie, lovely Jeannie, for me you needn't mourn
But the cruel stones now crush my bones, I'll never more return.'

As I rose in the morning, my dream was clarified:
The neighbours said, 'John Southern's dead,' and bitterly they
   cried.
'As he was working at his trade the roof upon him fell.'
The sorrow at my heart no mortal tongue can tell.

Come all you fair and pretty maids, a warning take by me;
Don't place your sweet affections at the top of any tree.
For once I loved a collier lad, and he loved me also;
But through the cruel mines he died and in his grave lies low.

Abigail Parkes didn't look straight at the collier as he sang. She seemed afraid to watch him directly. Instead she kept staring at the uncurtained window, which the dark night outside turned into a mirror. It showed no sign of little Susanna, who was squatting down below it on the window seat, only Abigail herself with the firelight reflecting on her golden hair, and the entranced singing miner. In the reflecting window she could study him, while she felt in her heart the prophetic sadness of the song he sang.

All this I thought I had written in my book. But a slight stir in the bedroom made me jump, and I came to my senses. I found my biro still fallen on the floor, and the notebook open on the edge of the bed. I must have been daydreaming, or even asleep perhaps. My reading lamp was out, but the light over the dressing table was switched on. By its dim light I saw a girl who looked at first like Abigail, staring away at her reflection in the dressing table mirror. I could see the back of her head and her reflected face, just as I had been doing before in my imagination.

'Oh, Jean,' I yawned. 'You didn't half make me jump. How long have you been sitting there?'

'I was going to brush my hair out, but I started thinking instead.'

'Yes. I'm glad your Steve is going to be a teacher, not a miner. It must be a dangerous life.'

'Well, I don't know how you knew that's what I was thinking about. Yes; though of course, the mines are all finished.'

'Not by the looks of our cabbage patch,' I said. 'They may have really finished, but we can't get rid of them.'

'Come to think of it, that's right about most things round here though. I never went much on history, Teresa, but you can't get rid of these things easily can you?'

'You can't at all,' I said. 'Once a thing happens, it makes a sort of bump in things, and you can't iron the bump out.'

Honestly, I don't know what I was on about. I felt at the time as though this was a sensible and wise thing to say, but perhaps it wasn't. I was very sleepy, and Jean had now picked up her hairbrush, so I knew she would be there for a long time.

'Sorry, Jean,' I murmured, 'but I'm absolutely dog tired. I'll just have to say good night.'

'OK, kiddo. See you in the morning.'

The morning was another day to meet my friends, to meet David, and to talk about Abigail. I shut my eyes tight to get there soon.

8

'Have We Started Something?'

I expect most schools are the same as ours, really, though I hope they aren't. In ours, it's not easy for girls and boys to talk without getting a label shoved round their necks. I dread any label like that, and I hate being teased. But I did want to see David that day and tell him what had happened to the Willetts cabbage patch. At break I nearly had a chance. Val was cheeking Kevin Bayliss about his hair, which was getting a bit long for the school rules. She hadn't got her eye on me.

I sidled along in David's direction, but almost at once Val was back, full of silly plans about what she was going to do to the Geography student we'd got, some poor wretched lad who wasn't doing Val any harm.

'I bet I can get him to go out with me,' she said. You'd have thought she'd got a licence to persecute him! About this time, I was getting mighty tired of wretched Val.

When school dinner finished, and the chairs had been scraped back under their tables ready for second sitting, I had another try. I pushed along the corridor behind him, trying to get within earshot among the jostling crowds.

'Dave!' I shouted. My voice bounced off the back of a fat fifth-form girl. 'David!'

This time his head turned, and I marvelled to see his eyes brighten. This sent a warm glow through me. Not everyone brightens up when they see me.

'I was looking for you,' he said.

'Well, I've been shouting you all up the corridor.'

'I've got that death certificate. That's good for the GPO, considering we only sent off on Sunday. It doesn't say much that's new, though.'

'It's only Thursday now,' I answered. 'It is good. I've got things to tell you, very odd things.' I was amazed to find that I couldn't look straight at him, and had to look at the floor. How silly can you get!

'Well, we'd better go out. We can't talk here. The death certificate's in my satchel.'

I collected my coat, eluded Val, and met Dave with his satchel over his shoulder outside the main entrance. This time walking up the drive with the lad felt even odder than before. I found we were talking for a time without me hearing a word that either of us said.

'It came this morning,' I finally heard him say.

He opened his satchel, and took out a buff envelope. Out of this he drew a black-edged form, a long folded piece of paper with signatures all over it and a bright red seal stamped on it. The words were typed, though I imagine the original would be in flowery Victorian handwriting. Here are the details:

When and where died:	10 December 1860 near Gosty Hill canal tunnel
Name and surname:	Abigail Parkes
Sex:	Female
Age:	17 years
Occupation:	—
Cause of death:	Suicide by drowning
Signature, description & residence of informant:	George Hayes Hinchliffe Coroner West Bromwich

I scanned the document from top to bottom, but nothing else appeared except the date of registration and the registrar's signature.

'Are you disappointed?' David asked.

'I don't know,' I answered. 'There's nothing new, of course. But it's proof. I sort of feel Abigail's a bit more real if you've got a document to prove it. I see the word "suicide" is there, large as life.'

'Bound to be, as the coroner himself informed the registrar. It'd be just a formality.'

He slipped the thin piece of paper back into its envelope, addressed to Mr David H. Ray, and was going to put it back in his satchel.

'Could I keep it a bit?' I suddenly found myself asking.

'Yes, if you want to,' he answered, surprised. And there I was clutching the envelope in a sweaty hand, without the least knowing what I wanted it for. As a sort of pledge of Abigail, I suppose.

'Did you get back all right last night?' he asked me.

'Oh, yes. That brings it back. I meant to tell you. Yesterday our cabbages all fell into an old mine shaft, and you'll never guess what mine shaft it was.'

'I remember you brought a trade token your dad found there to the meeting last Thursday,' he answered.

I thought of last Thursday, and how it seemed worlds away.

'Yes. Well, an old chap that lives in our road says it was Fiery Holes, the one where David Caddick worked, remember? Before he went to the Black Bank? It was in the inquest.'

'Yes. And it caved in yesterday?'

'Mmm. All our cabbages were uprooted, and it was very lucky Dad or Mom wasn't there. We had the fire-brigade, police, everyone. As I came out this morning a newspaper reporter had just caught up with us.'

'Fell in through subsidence,' he mumbled to himself. 'You might have been there yourself. I'd have been sorry.'

'Yes, but David: was it just chance? The very same pit, I mean?'

'Eh?' He seemed not to know what I was on about.

'I mean, we aren't half getting mixed up with this Abigail. We keep on coming across things which have got something to do with her. She seems to keep happening, somehow.'

He didn't say anything to this, just shuffled his feet thoughtfully.

'Odd things, too,' I continued. 'We've had the gravestone, and the writing in the register . . .'

'Well, I didn't see that,' he put in.

'And then there was the inquest, and the death certificate . . .'

'But we found those on purpose!'

'But not this about the cabbages. Then, you see, I keep on dreaming about her. Last night again, just the same. If it is dreaming. And Jean says I talked in my sleep. Is it dangerous? Do you think we've somehow started something, you and me?'

'What?' he asked, looking surprised.

'Oh, I don't know. Could be anything. There seems to be something spooky, haunting, about it all.'

'I don't know about you, Teresa. We've been all through this haunting business before. Honestly, you can't be serious?'

'Well, what's it all about then?'

'How should I know? I know ghosts can't hurt you. That's for sure. Perhaps it's just that when you start taking an interest in the past you find yourself imagining more clearly than you'd expect.'

'I want to know about her,' I said violently. 'I want to find out why the poor girl felt so driven. And yet I get frightened, Dave. Can't you see, I really am bothered? I feel like finding out with you, and yet I get scared. I was yesterday at the inquest, though you mightn't know it.'

David sighed. 'I'm sure you've no need to get so worked

up. What is there to be scared about? It's all perfectly logical.'

'I don't know, really.' I found myself stuttering. 'It's just that ... she seems to take over. It doesn't ... it doesn't seem quite in my control.'

Of course, this was a very silly conversation. I was only making matters worse because David obviously wanted to be comforting, but had no idea what I was talking about. I'm not surprised; he probably couldn't understand me at all.

'By the way,' he said, changing the subject. 'You did say you'd show me that sampler one day. That's a good bit of evidence. There might be more in that than we've seen yet ... But look,' he went on, changing the tone of his voice, 'this Abigail hunt doesn't really matter. We've got on very well with it. We don't seem to squabble, and we've found out a lot. Truly, if you want to give it up, I don't mind. I can go on by myself.'

'No you can't,' I said harshly. 'You haven't seen the sampler. I'll have to help.'

'I'd miss your help, of course,' he said a bit shyly. 'But what's on the sampler?'

'Oh, the actual words aren't very exciting. Just some quotations out of the Bible, and an alphabet with a few flowers on. Mind, they're very bright and shimmering. Yellow, they are. Gorse, if you know what that is.'

'Of course I do,' he answered. 'It's funny how gorse keeps going. It's supposed to flower all the year. You can see it any time, you know, even January. And it's almost impossible to kill gorse. You can divide it, and dig coal and limestone all round it, you can build houses all over it, but you can't kill it. It's still all over the place round here, even though there are houses everywhere these days.'

'I know. And very prickly it can be,' I replied. 'There's some at the bottom of our garden by the railway cutting. If you try to squeeze through it to see the trains, you've had it. You can get it in the neck—in fact, everywhere. But I love the flowers, they're so gay and bright.'

A large splodge of rain fell on my head.

'Cuss. It's raining. Better turn back,' I said. The clouds ahead were looking dark and bulging, and it began to seem as though the calm, mild spell of the past week was over.

'It's just my luck, you know, David. I'm doing a friend's paper round tonight for her. It looks like being a wet evening. I just cannot abide water in any shape or form.'

'Oh, I don't know,' said David. 'You can make it into tea, or even pop.'

'It won't rain pop though. Only cold rain, down my neck.'

'Well, don't say that about water. I'd like to see Thimblemill Baths without any water. Folks'd have a job swimming.'

'I can't swim and I won't.' I edged away from the explosive topic, by going back to an earlier conversation. 'What are you doing here, then, if you say you come from Cheshire? What a strange place to come from!'

'What's strange about it? It seems stranger to me to think of all you Black Country people living in the same place for centuries, intermarrying and never moving. That's what I call strange.'

At this point we had to give up all hope of talking and dash back along the lane as fast as we could to school. The rain started to teem from the sky, and there were no houses or shops to shelter by. We raced along, never stopping until we came to the school door, where by custom we must part, for girls went one way and boys another. A sprightly and smirking Val was there to welcome me back. But I'd reached breaking point with her. Not waiting to hear her taunts, I disappeared quickly into the toilets.

9
On the Canal Bridge

The paper round went badly. I didn't know the order of the houses, as I was doing this for a girl called Stephanie, who lives in the next road. I was wearing an anorak which kept away most of the rain from my body, but not off my legs or out of my shoes. The dark had closed in before tea. You couldn't call this autumn any more, it was definitely winter. Oh, how I wish people would put the number on their house nice and clear, so that it can be seen from the road. And I wish they'd all buy themselves larger letter-boxes for Christmas. Any paper boy or girl'd support me on this.

I traipsed round the estate, weighed down by the sack and not daring to leave it. When I got down to Slack Hillock by the canal, there was a great big puddle under the railway bridge. Just as I was going past it, a car rushed through at forty miles an hour, splashing freezing mud all up my legs. I felt more than a bit gloomy.

My last *Express and Star* of the evening was to be dropped in at the Sportsman pub, and I crossed the canal to take it. The bridge isn't a hump-backed one now, but an iron-framed bridge put up during the 1880s. The evening was so wet I didn't notice the bridge on my way over. My thoughts were miles away, I don't know where. But on my way back it occurred to me that I might as well stop and have a look at the exact place where Abigail pitched herself in, that far off night.

I stopped and looked over the rail. There were street

lights now, which there hadn't been in those days. But there weren't any boats on the canal, whether you looked past the bridge which serves our estate to the black mouth of Gosty Hill tunnel, or towards the bend where the canal goes by the factory and under Waterfall Lane. The names round our way seem pretty, I'll agree. 'Gosty Hill' means the hill of gorse, really, and sometimes I think of lovely yellow clumps by a swift clear waterfall. I suppose there was one there once, but now it's chiefly known for an industrial estate and a roadmenders' yard. Still, by the Sportsman, it does look a bit like country even now—our sort of country, with the roads, canals, and railways crossing each other among the yellowing grasses and scattered hawthorns, which are a brilliant magical white in June. But now it was drear November, and the hawthorns rust brown.

I looked down into the dark water, with the raindrops breaking and spoiling my reflection. In any case it looked pale in the creamy-orange corporation light. I could have been looking into an ancient mirror with cracks across it, only the cracks formed and reformed themselves as I looked. The blackness behind my rain-lashed face as I stared at it in the water reminded me of the blackness I had seen in my dream the night before as Abigail had gazed into the reflecting window to watch David the collier sing. Then, as I stood contemplating, there appeared in the dark water something which caused my heart to thump and made me catch my breath. If I could have distinguished shades of pink in the reflection down there, I'd certainly have seemed paler, very pale.

Very, very slowly, like the image of some teacher's fingers on a screen when they creep in to move a picture on an epidiascope, there moved into my field of vision another face. It seemed propelled, like a puppet, by something outside itself. Like my own reflection it was broken

by the raindrops spattering. It was pale and yet clear, the
face of a young girl whose sharp dark eyes I could just dis-
tinguish. I froze completely, and felt utterly sick. The
girl must be just behind and beside me, looking into the
canal over my shoulder. She had neither spoken to me nor
touched me, but she could not be half an inch away. Any
second she might touch me, and I should collapse. I tried
to see her out of the corner of my eye without moving my
head, but couldn't quite manage it. I gazed back into the
blackness of the canal, wondering what the beautiful girl
behind me would do. I simply dursn't move a muscle or
bat an eyelid. Apart from the spattering rain there was no
sound, for tonight was windless.

This was the most terrifying thing that happened to me
in all those days of curiosity about Abigail, and I'm sure
it need not have terrified me. But at the time I didn't
know how to break the deadlock. I could not have turned
round 'for a pension', as they say. So I might be there
still, except that an extra large drop of rain hurtled at that
moment into the reflected face in the canal, producing a
perfectly formed ring in the centre of her forehead, which
spread till her face was quite surrounded by a clear circular aura. It was like the old pictures I've seen of saints
in the Middle Ages. I heard myself give a tremendous
sigh and turned, suddenly released, to see what I had
partly expected—there was no one behind at all.

Then I was off like a hare to the paper shop with my
empty bag. I couldn't see straight, and I had a stitch in
my side as I ran. How stupid I'd been! I had toyed and
played with a dragon in searching for Abigail. I'd thought
it was fun to follow David in his quest. A full week we'd
spent, trailing the story of this distant girl and forgetting
everything else. The quest had taken hold of my heart;
with David as fellow plotter I'd lived years in a short week.
Now I realised that Abigail was no toy to be played with,

no fiction. It wasn't like 'creative writing' at school where I could stop when I wanted. If I did not drop the whole thing now, it might involve me too much. Then it would be too late to stop.

But how should I break this to David? He wouldn't understand. Abigail's spell on him was of a different kind altogether, and I could never explain myself to him. A sickly resolve took hold of me, that tomorrow I must act as if he didn't exist, or as if he were no more involved in my affairs than any other person in the school. In panic I determined, cross my heart and hope to die, that from now on there should be no Abigail, no David Caddick, no David Ray.

When I got home from the paper round I ate my tea in a dream. Mom was still flapping about the cabbages, and she never noticed. I suppose I must have been shocked or something by seeing the face in the canal, and I just couldn't seem to settle despite my determination to put the whole thing out of my mind. As soon as I possibly could, I escaped from the tea table and sidled off round the door into the hall, meaning to go upstairs and get on with my homework.

But in the hall was Abigail's sampler. It suddenly seemed horrid, and on an impulse I climbed on a chair, turned it round to face the wall, then off I went leaving a brown paper-covered object to greet anyone who might glance at it. By the time I came to look at it again, which was about three o'clock in the middle of Friday night, it was facing the front again. But how that came about, I don't know at all. I never touched it, I'm sure.

I quickly settled the homework, concentrating furiously. It was a big relief to get it done, and to look at the pile of biro-written scribble that emerged in answer to a question in History. Then I started to repack my satchel for Friday morning. While I was doing this, I came across a thin buff envelope, the sight of which sent my mind into a fury of hatred.

The envelope said 'Mr David H. Ray'. Inside was a black-edged document which I snatched out impatiently. It reminded me cruelly of what I was trying to forget: and I felt that I deserved to be allowed forgetfulness. I certainly yearned for some rest both from Mr Ray and Miss Parkes. I hated them both, for both seemed to want to control me, and threatened my private self, which I didn't intend to be touched. No one will ever tell me what I can and can't do.

In an icy temper I yanked at the buff envelope with my fingernails. It wouldn't rip. I folded it over, so that I couldn't see the name and address, nor the black-bordered end of the death certificate protruding from it. I tugged at it again, with desperate force. This time it ripped right across. I folded it again, and again it ripped. I tore the fragments twice more, till the buff envelope and death certificate were in no bigger pieces than confetti at a wedding. Then into the firegrate with the lot! I jumped back on to my bed with my heart thumping.

A little later I crept back to the edge of the bed, looked over, and saw the remains of the paper littering the empty fireplace. Immediately I raced down to the kitchen, grabbed a box of matches, flew upstairs again, struck three of them and lit a brilliant miniature bonfire in the bare coaly grate. With three matches burning the paper crackled, browned and disappeared into smoke and ash within a minute. 'So perish David Ray and Abigail Parkes,' I said dramatically aloud. 'I am free of them both.'

I bounded back to the bed again, slung off my satchel on to the floor and hurled my shoes after it. All my school books scattered to the four corners of the room as the satchel sped along; and they lay crumpled and untidy where they fetched up, against walls, chairs and Jean's dressing table. Hate and fury ran riot in me as I lay on the bed, and what thoughts came into my head I don't remember. I wished the fire in the grate had burnt the house down and me with it ... I don't know what I wished. Of course, it was mad, crazy, destructive, horrible. Yes, yes, I was sorry afterwards for all this wild temper. But at the time I was bitterly glad that I had wiped out Abigail and David at one go.

10

Water and Fire

Each time an important thing has happened in my life I have felt afraid about what it would lead to. I was like this at age four when we moved from our little old house in Old Hill into the council house, and it was the same when I passed the eleven-plus. The thing that happened was exciting in itself, but I was afraid, and wanted to go back to before it happened. Seeing the face of Abigail in the dark canal was the same, and I spent the next few days trying desperately to get back to myself before I'd seen her. I felt as if a new Teresa had been born, and I wanted the old one back. I suppose that's why I tried so hard to tell someone else about the ghost in the water, so that they'd either convince me really and truly that it never happened, or else they'd make sense of it for me.

By now, in my mind, I was calling it 'the ghost in the water'. There was still a puzzle though, because I had almost felt the girl with her burning blue eyes near my shoulder. Yet somehow, she was 'in the water' too. I had looked down, craning over the bridge, and she was there. But as I turned round quickly, I knew she had almost touched my arm. It was all very muddling, and when I tried to reason it out, it seemed logically that what I had felt was a ghost, and what I had seen only the reflection of a ghost. And how could I ever explain this to anyone?

I knew better than to try telling Val when I saw her on Friday. Instead, I sat on the bus with her in total boredom while she regaled me with a long tale of what she had done the night before, rushing about on the motorway with her cousins in a hotted up banger. A little part of me wished I was like her, to get pleasure out of speed and a whirl of people. But even though I hated Abigail, I had to admit to myself that I didn't want to be like Val, not really. I blushed for shame when she told me her day's plans for the Geography student.

By the time I reached the form room, I was determined to say something about last night, even if no one understood. At least if that happened, I could have a lovely sulk, and imagine myself wronged, lonely and misunderstood. Val had gone on ahead, and was talking to David when I opened the door. The only other person in the room was the slow-witted girl, Tracy Dobbs. She was the one who had brought her sampler to the local history club the week before, and started it all off.

'Well, I saw a ghost last night,' I began shyly.

The story was soon told and plainly told, and I knew I had got nowhere. No one believed me. It was as though the fiery flame of my experience had been snuffed out against a blank wall of asbestos.

'. . . so it was a ghost. It was her ghost, Abigail's. That's what I saw,' I finished.

'It couldn't be a ghost really,' David said kindly. This morning he was a hundred miles from me; his kindness infuriated me—distant, polite, uncomprehending kindness.

'I mean, I'm not saying you didn't see something . . .' he rattled on.

'More than you'll ever see,' I shouted out rudely. 'You can't even see what's right in front of your nose.'

'Ghosts now,' interrupted Val. 'Really, Teresa, that's the laugh of the century! No one can see ghosts! You've been watching too much Scooby Doo on telly.'

Of course, I knew it would be like this. But I didn't care: I wanted not to be understood.

David tried again. Evidently he hadn't noticed the rudeness of my reply to him.

'You see, Teresa, there aren't such things. There couldn't be, really.' Know-all David, kind and distant, talking to me as if I was an imbecile five-year-old.

'Hoo . . . ooo . . . ooo!' wailed Val, wide-eyed. 'I suppose it had clanking chains?'

I dug her hard in the ribs with my elbow, and told her to get lost. As for Tracy Dobbs, she stood fidgeting in the background, swinging one foot backwards and forwards. She never said a thing, and it wasn't till days later that she gave me a clue to her thoughts.

By the time I got home on Friday night, I'd gone all babyish and wanted to tell Mom all about everything, but I just couldn't seem to find the chance. She was worrying on about the mess the workmen were making while they tried to fill in the old mine shaft, and complaining of the cups of tea they were drinking. In the end I gave that attempt up too, and went upstairs hoping to get something out of Jean's transistor.

And in fact there was something a bit consoling. My kind of music is folksy. I can't bear Bach and all those people that David likes, and I don't really care that much for pop either, thought I wouldn't tell Val that. But I'm crazy about Irish dance tunes and that sort of way-out stuff. And this particular night there was a programme of 'folk' which included a ballad sung to a gorgeous eerie tune by a solo girl singer. I had heard it before, and in fact knew it quite well. It ought to have given me a bit of help in understanding Abigail, but I missed the clue for a good while.

The song is called 'Broken Token'. It is about a soldier going to the war. He gives his girl-friend a ring—or in many versions half a ring—as a token before he leaves for the field of battle. Years later, when she thinks he's dead,

he comes back. She has been mourning for him, and stayed
loyal all the while. At first, when she meets him by the side
of a river, she can't recognise him. He tries to tempt her
without saying who he is and promises gold, jewels, a high
castle to live in, everything. But she says no, she is promised
to her dear William, who went away to the wars.

> 'What care I for your high, high castle
> All decorated with lilies white?
> Oh, what care I for your gold and silver
> If my dear William were here tonight?'

When he hears this, the happy soldier takes out of his
pocket his half of the broken ring. The girl instantly
recognises his real self through the dirt, grey hairs, beard,
damaged leg or whatever he's got which he didn't have
when he went away. They fall in love all over again and this
time are happily married. I thought to myself as I listened
how powerful loyalty to a loved one could be, and how it
was all summed up in the magic of that golden ring.

I fell asleep quickly that night. But somewhere in the
small hours I woke up in a panic. I had dreamt that smoke
was billowing round the bedroom, and that when I went
to the window to look out and see where it came from the
whole of Gosty Hill was alight. Snakes of fire scuttered
through the grass and overwhelmed the gorse, which sizzled
up into nothing like cellophane on a bonfire. I could smell
the smoke, almost, when I woke up. I couldn't see flames in
the room, but I didn't trust the railway bank not to be
alight. So I hopped out of bed to look through the window.

To my surprise, all the world outside was silver-grey
with a fey, shimmering light. I realised that the moon was
shining on frost that had formed everywhere. Somehow I
had forgotten that when I looked out I should see the houses
of the estate. I was expecting the open scrubby land of the

last century, the pit banks and the colliery fordroughs, the gins which horses used to pull to wind up the cages. Nothing seemed to move outside, and I thought perhaps the whole world had died in the night, leaving me as sole survivor. Jean had not come in, and I supposed that if the world really had died, she never would do. I had no idea what the time was.

On an impulse I opened the door and went downstairs. That's something I never do, nor does anyone else in our house. We all sleep soundly. There was deep silence as I slipped down the treads in my bare feet, and I didn't know what was leading me down. I could see the hall black and silver-grey; the moon seemed better at lighting it than the sun. Why I went, I still don't know. I wasn't calm, like the still moonlight, but agitated, as if from the touch of fire in my dream.

In the hall hung the sampler. Like a girl in a trance, I stared up at it on tiptoe, forgetting that it should still have been face to the wall. As if I didn't know well enough what it said, I spelt the letters out again. *CAST YOUR BREAD UPON THE WATERS. LET HIM WHO IS WITH-OUT SIN CAST THE FIRST STONE.* The twisted, spiky Gothic letters stood out, grey upon grey. My feet were cold, and I shivered as I stood there. I was quite mithered about this writing, which seemed like some power of enchantment, dazzling me. Was it the sampler which had drawn me down the stairs in the depth of night and the cool frosty moonlight, to give me instruction or let me into some secret? I glared at it and worried about it. Even then I didn't remember that the night before I'd turned it round to face the wall.

Suddenly the front door grated open. My nerve gave way, and I heard myself give a sob of shock. It was really uncanny, the door opening by itself. I felt as if I must be going to see the ghostly face I had seen on Thursday

evening stealthily appear. But no, the door was not opening
by itself. Jean was quietly pushing it, so as not to disturb
anyone. When she had it some way open, she poked her
head round and looked in at me. I knew what would
happen. She bellowed out a noise like a factory bull.

'Shut up!' I warned. 'They'll hear.'

She clapped her hand over her mouth, and actually they
didn't hear.

'What the hell are you doing, Tess?' she asked in a tone
I couldn't quite analyse. Cross? Shocked? Conspiratorial?
Quiet, anyway.

'I'm just . . . I'm not doing anything,' I hissed.

'It's that sampler. I've seen you at it before. I suppose it
was you that turned it back to front yesterday. If you keep
standing there without a dressing gown on, you'll get that
on you as you won't get off.'

'I don't know what made me come down. I don't really.
I had a dream about fire . . . All the gorse was on fire.'

'All what gorse?' She had a point there. The view from
our bedroom is mostly council houses.

'Look,' she went on. 'I'm dog tired and it's very late. If
I don't get into that bed soon I shall meet myself coming
back. Do you mind if we go upstairs and finish up there?
I tell you, Teresa, life is hell.'

'I know,' I said. 'I've been wondering if it's because I'm
not casting any bread on the waters.'

'Casting *what*?' Jean asked, and I don't blame her.

One after the other we crept up to bed like guilty mice. I
jumped in quickly, but Jean wouldn't go to bed until she'd
brushed her hair. In the moonlight it was shiny as gos-
samer, and she might have been a fairy-tale princess. I
yawned, but said nothing. The wristwatch by my bedside
told me it was nearly three o'clock, a horrible hour.

'The sampler says "cast your bread upon the waters",' I
said.

'Yes,' she answered, 'and the ducks get it all before the swan.' She moved away from the mirror and I could hear her getting into bed.

'Sleepy?' she asked.

'Not now,' I replied, yawning.

'You would be if you'd danced your feet off like me, then argued till you don't know if you're coming or going. Some folk I know would swear black's white.'

' "You could make me believe, with your lying tongue, that the sun rose in the west",' I quoted from a ballad.

'You've said it, Tess. However, I'm here all right. I'm careful where I cast my bread. And we are not getting married before a certain young fellow finishes college. So what's your trouble?'

'I think I'm going daft,' I replied. 'And I'm never getting married. Never. Never. All this love: it only makes people drown themselves.'

Jean ignored the second part of my outburst.

'You could be at that. Going daft, I mean. Standing in the cold hall gawping at an old relic at half two in the morning.'

'You see, Jean. The person who made that sampler . . . I saw her on Thursday night, and I think . . . I don't know what I think.'

'Oh yes? She'd be about a hundred and forty, would she? Or only a hundred and thirty?' Jean's satire was cutting, but perhaps it was what I needed.

'She only seemed young.'

'And if I recall, on Wednesday you had an exciting evening in the city library, digging up something. You don't think you live too much in the past, Tess? As I said before, the past's still with us, but perhaps it's better to let sleeping dogs lie.'

'Well, you see, David found out about the past by working things out. He thought, and he found evidence, and so on. It was my job to imagine. They say I'm better at that.'

' "David found", not "finds"? He's finished then?'

'As far as I care. It's all finished. He's finished, and the sampler.'

'It looks like it, with you standing there at half two frozen to death.'

'I haven't spoken to him all day.' She said nothing to that, and I must admit it rather surprised me to hear myself say it.

'But I did hear a song about a soldier coming back from the war to find his true love faithful.'

'Could be just a song,' said cynical Jean. She gave a yawn and snuggled tight into her bed.

As for me, I felt I might tear the clothes into little bits. Instead, I chewed a button off my pyjamas. All through that silly conversation, I felt there was more to tell Jean, somehow, but I just didn't know what. When I got back to sleep, things were no better. My dreams contained fire again, and blackest gloom. I was very glad when day dawned.

11

What are Ghosts?

On Saturday mornings, I generally used to go shopping in Blackheath with Val. This particular Saturday, I forced myself to go and call for her as usual, despite her rudeness the day before. But all she did was to shout taunts at me out of her bedroom window, and I'm sorry to say I gave up in disgust and went home to get the week-end homework done.

By the afternoon I was simply bored with everything. I was neither cross nor tearful nor frightened. I didn't hate anyone, I didn't love anyone. I was just bored. I decided to catch a bus out to the country, to a hill where I could get a bit of peace and no one would ask me what I was doing if I acted peculiar. So I toiled up to the top of Gosty Hill and waited by the tube works for a number 217. On the ride, and walking up the lane afterwards to the top of the green hill, I pretended I was being followed. I kept looking at all the people on the bus, wondering which one could be out of another century, keeping an eye on me to see I didn't learn too much. When I got off at the terminus, I didn't walk straight up the little lane to the top of the hill, but dodged along ditches, through hedges and behind trees to throw off any possible pursuer.

Just as I neared the top of the hill, sounds of pursuit began to register in real life; there was a heavy panting behind me which at first made me afraid to turn round. Yet all the while, I knew my reluctance was a game, not real like the ghost of Abigail had been. I knew that when I did turn round, I'd find some perfectly good explanation of the panting, and that whether I turned round or not, nothing odd was going to happen. I was trying to pretend fear when I wasn't scared, but I couldn't work up much enthusiasm for it. The truth was, I suppose, that boredom still had me in its grip. 'Go on, look round. I dare you,' I said to myself. And I accepted the dare.

Immediately I recognised Mr Milner, the vicar at David's church. It was not he who was doing the panting, but a shaggy mongrel dog which was wandering along a few yards behind me, snuffling in mud and round tree stumps. The vicar himself was a hundred yards or so further back, but in spite of the distance, he recognised me and waved a friendly hand. There seemed nothing for it but to take a rest on the grass by the side of the path and wait for him. I didn't want to be rude, even though vicars have no interest for me.

'I thought I knew you,' Mr Milner said, as he dropped on the damp grass beside me. 'My, it takes some puff to climb up here.'

'Yes,' I agreed rather sharply.

He sat for a while staring at the distant view over the Black Country and fondling the black and white mongrel. Its great big tongue was hanging out, and it was still panting little puffs of steam into the wintry air.

'How's the quest? I suppose you're Dr Watson and David's Sherlock?'

'Could be,' I mumbled non-committally. In the quiet of my heart, I disagreed. But what was the sense in saying so? If I explained, we'd soon be on Abigail again, and of course that was the last thing I wanted.

'I rather like a walk round the graveyard myself,' the vicar went on. 'And quite often I find myself wondering about the lives and deaths of all those people. I must admit, I wouldn't like to see all the gravestones flattened. They hold a lot of history. Some people would like to grass over all churchyards, or turn them into car parks.'

At first, when he sat down, I thought he might be a nuisance. But he seemed a friendly soul, not stuck up at all. Perhaps he might be useful. Perhaps he might answer me some questions.

'Could I ask you something?' I ventured, not looking at him. His face was still like David's in old age.

'You can try. But I don't suppose I'll have a sensible answer. I'd better throw a stick for Josh here, or he'll think I don't care. Half a minute.'

He got to his feet and found a few stones, one of which he hurled away across the stretch of turf. The dog rushed after it, skithering round on the yielding grass, and finally picked up the stone in his soft jaws.

'Plenty of stones, but no sticks,' he said, throwing another. 'What is it, then?'

'It's about suicide,' I began doubtfully. 'Is it a very bad crime?'

'Wait a bit, that's a snorter,' he answered, sitting down heavily on the grass again. 'I mean, "crime" hardly seems the word, does it? Once it's done, they can't put you on trial, can they? No mortal judge, I mean?'

'No . . .' This was obvious.

'Then again, I don't see it's a crime to feel suicidal. I am, often, when I hear the congregation's singing some Sundays. No one's tried me for it yet, though, because I've never told anyone. It's easy to feel suicidal.'

'You can say that again,' I agreed.

'Heartfelt! But of course, doing it's another matter. You'd only reach that stage if you had an iron will or were out of your mind, I'd say.'

'Abigail's supposed to have done it, according to the coroner. You know, the girl we're finding out about. Or were . . .'

'Oh? You looked up the inquest, did you?'

'Yes. On Wednesday night.'

'It would be very bad for her relatives if she did commit suicide.'

'Yes. But I've got this feeling that she didn't. The coroner said she did. I don't know what happened, but I just don't feel sure about the suicide. And her father wasn't sure. He seemed determined to believe she hadn't.'

'You might be able to find out what kind of a girl she was,' the vicar mused.

It was in for a penny, in for a pound. 'I know she wasn't that kind of girl, to kill herself,' I answered. 'I think I've seen her ghost,' I added dully.

He never turned a hair. It made me wonder what some people tell him, if even a ghost was nothing to bother about.

'It was down on the bridge where she died. Last Thursday. It was terrible. It's put me off completely. I just want no more to do with it all, I'm afraid.'

'Well, if you feel happier to leave it . . .'

'No. That's the trouble. I don't feel happier. I feel much unhappier, truly. I can't go on, because I'm scared; and I can't not go on, because I get a feeling of loneliness and having run away.'

'And what does David say? About the ghost, I mean, and about your feelings?'

'I dursn't tell him. I haven't even seen him. He doesn't know what I'm up to,' I said in a rush. 'He must think I'm horrible, a deserter.'

'You mean you never told him about seeing this girl?'

'No,' I said. Whatever was it, that made me tell a lie even when I was trying to gets things straightened out?

'For all you know,' the vicar said slowly and judiciously, 'this Abigail needs your help to put things straight. And David too. He can't work it all through without you. At least you must talk it over with him or you are a deserter. And isn't that kind of giving up a bit like suicide? I think you need to fight a bit, old lady.'

I was a bit surprised at being called 'old lady', but I tried to take it kindly.

'Even if she did kill herself, the girl was probably out of her mind. Can't you find out why and lay the ghost? I think you must go on with your quest; you have to.'

'It's all either silly as hell, or dead serious,' I said. 'And I can't seem to know which.'

'Almost a crusade,' he answered. For the first time he looked at me, a little curiously, I thought. I can't imagine what I looked like, but I must have been very untidy and dirty. Dead leaves and sticks were all over me, from dodging through hedges. My face was healthily red, I suppose, but smeared with some lipstick that I'd put on during the morning to cheer myself up.

'Could I ask how you came? Not on a bike, I suppose?' he asked.

'On a 217 bus, then along the lane.'

'That must have taken a time. An hour or so, I'll bet.'

'I don't know.'

'Well, if you feel like going back now, my girl, I'll give you a lift in the Mini. Come on, Josh!' He stood up and whistled to the dog.

I did begin to feel like going back, to tell the truth. I had got the clear hill air in my lungs. I began to see answers to my questions, though there were a whole lot more crowding in. The vicar was right when he said that David and Abigail both relied on me, and I had to go back prepared to get involved in things again. The pale moonlight I had seen last night came back to my mind. It was all so still, and very beautiful. You couldn't want the moonlight for ever, though, nor even the clear hill air. Sooner or later you had to go back to the bustling brightness of the towns, to meet and deal with the people there and get mixed up with them.

I led the way down the path again to the car park, and we climbed into the vicar's Mini. Josh jumped into the back seat and sat down obediently on the rug.

'He's a car dog,' the vicar said. 'Not a lap dog, a car dog.'

The rutted mud of the car park was left behind us, and we started down the lane towards home.

'I don't know what ghosts are, Teresa,' he went on. 'But I don't rule them out. I was brought up on angels, which you probably think are a very foolish idea.'

'Yes,' I said quickly.

'I thought you might.'

'I didn't mean to be rude,' I interposed, probably blushing.

'That's all right. You're entitled to your opinion. What I was going to say was, if angels, why not ghosts?'

'Both a kind of hallucination?' I suggested.

'Whatever a hallucination is,' he answered. 'Plenty of people have thought they saw things other people didn't see. Joan of Arc reckoned she could hear them, too. And they don't always tell people wrong. So I'll accept your ghost if you like.'

I was very grateful indeed, but I felt a trap nearing. If he agreed to my ghost, I felt I should agree to his angel. But that I certainly would not do. Worse might follow; we might get anywhere. There was a quiet five minutes in the car, while I argued with my conscience. It was playing me up no end, talking very persuasively.

'I don't suppose anyone quite knows what's what,' said the vicar, breaking the silence. 'Doubtless we clergy sometimes pretend to more knowledge than we're certain of. We start off being sure of the basic points, and then we let them go hard inside us, and forget that the longer you live the more you can understand if you mean to.'

'I don't absolutely say there isn't some kind of God,' I was surprised to hear myself say. 'But I can't believe in angels, that's all.'

'I'll tell you what, though,' he answered. 'I'll be interested to know the result of your quest. Don't forget to let me know.'

He dropped me off at the top of Gosty Hill, where I had got on the bus earlier. I ran down the slope to our house in a happy whirl, empty-headed and free-hearted. Abigail's bridge didn't hold any terror now, and I waved to it as I passed. I found I was looking forward excitedly to Monday. If only David could forgive my Friday rudeness, I should love to talk the whole thing over, and he'd just have to believe me.

The front gate slammed to behind me. I marched up the path, avoiding the debris from Fiery Holes mine. I was late again, but glad to be home.

12

Seagulls Inland

Monday morning brought a shimmering white frost. I woke up early, thinking it was snow. I was early out of the house on my way to school, too. I wanted to walk, not go on the school bus with Val. Val would spoil what Mr Milner had said, and make me doubt myself. As it turned out, my instinct to walk was right, and I found my belief in the ghost supported, not weakened.

Instead of meeting Val, I ran straight into Tracy Dobbs, and groaned inwardly. Tracy lives in a terrace house which backs on to some small factories. It has escaped being knocked down in 'slum clearance' so far, though a wilderness of broken bricks and willow herb surrounds it. Tracy was just coming out of the entry, a carrier bag in her hand instead of a satchel. She had a beret too small for her stuck on the side of her gingery hair, and her grey eyes lit with surprise when she saw me.

'Hullo. What brings you this way?'

'Just fancied a walk,' I mumbled.

'Oh, strike! I've left me Maths book,' she exclaimed, and dashed back to get it. 'Don't wait!' she shouted over her shoulder. There was some other comment too, lost in the banging of the entry door. I was very tempted to do as she said and go on, but it seemed mean. I hung about for her on the footpath, but I wasn't looking forward to the walk any more.

'Here we am!' she yelled as she came back. She seemed so common with her slangy talk, I wished I had gone on ahead.

'Wouldn't do to leave the Maths behind,' she said with a wink. 'Have me in jug, he would.' By this she meant detention.

We walked along in silence, past the old concrete railway halt, now a ruin, past the crumbling brickwork of a demolished bridge, and up a long slope towards the canal, where the gas works used to be. Not a word did either of us speak. I was too edgy, and, as for Tracy, she seemed to ruminate, like a cow.

'You was on about ghosts on Friday,' she began hesitantly, as we crossed the canal and went down the other side of the slope towards the council's exhibition roundabout. In summer it's quite pretty, all flowers and shrubs.

I didn't want to talk about ghosts at all.

'Me dad saw one. In a dream you know,' Tracy said.

'No?' I said, interest flickering.

'He used to work up the quarries.' She meant the huge roadstone quarry that burrows deep into the heart of Turner's Hill, where the men at the bottom look so small you'd think they were little plasticene models.

'Well, this one night he had an awful dream. It was a visitation. His dad—that'd be my grandad—come to him and told him not to go. The fuse was goin' t'explode before its time. The vision told him some men'd be killed. It's Gospel truth, Tess.'

I didn't say anything, though by now I was interested.

'Mom told him not to be so saft. Her said not to believe in ghosts and the like. But Dad, well, he is saft. He'll study hunches and all sorts. He said he wasn't goin'. Well, that day, the fuse never went wrong at all. So nothin' bad happened to the men. But me dad was still dubious, like. He never went to work at all that week, and on the Friday he was proved right. A face of rock fell in which everyone thought was firm, and sure enough two men were buried and died under it. You don't believe me, do you, any more than Val or David believed you? It's Gospel, though, as I say.'

'I think I do, Tracy,' I answered. 'I really think I do. But don't ask me why, because I don't know.'

'Your Val Higgins, her'd never believe you, you know.'

'I know,' I answered. 'She's supposed to be my best friend. But she's no help at all. All she does is keep borrowing homework off me and getting us both into trouble.'

'Her's got green eyes.'

'No, brown,' I contradicted.

'They might look brown, but they'm got green in 'em.'

The penny dropped. Val was jealous, she meant. But what of?

'You'm beatin' her, see? All ways at once.'

I suddenly found Tracy interesting, despite her tactless ways.

'Now, what about you, Tracy? I don't notice you being top of the form. But you don't seem to get so cross as Val.'

'Well, I know I'm hopeless. Schoolwork—it don't interest me whatever I do.'

'But don't you mind doing subjects you don't understand?'

'Like Physics you mean? No. I'll soon be finished with school. One subject's as good as another; I never let them bother me.'

'David's a genius at Physics,' I said, thinking aloud.

'You want to tell him things slow. He'd believe you if you did. You looked right miserable on Friday, Tess.'

At first I thought this was a cheek. Tracy is offensive, there's no doubt.

'I've told you me dad saw a ghost,' she went on, her tone persuasive. I said nothing, and you could hear us both breathing heavily as we climbed the steep road towards the school.

'That's why he's still alive,' she persisted. There was another pause.

'You never spoke to David after Friday-before-school,' she said again. 'I saw you not looking at him.'

'I felt a fool,' I admitted.

'Better try again today,' she said. 'Trust your Aunt Tracy. Remember, David's clever. Clever folk don't like ghosts, dreams, anything. You don't even like the one you saw yourself, only you're honest.'

'Yes. I'm going to try again, anyway.'

'See them seagulls up there?' A flock of white birds was flapping and wheeling up in the sky. I hadn't noticed them before. They looked lovely and carefree as the weak winter sun caught their silvery feathers.

'Seagulls, are they?' I asked, surprised.

'Yes. Now, I'll bet if I asked at school this morning how many folk saw seagulls on their way to school, the whole lot'd say no. But they've all sid them really.'

'Mmm?'

'They *know*, you see. They know seagulls are what you see at Weston, or Rhyl. They don't believe in seagulls inland, and they'm not able to see 'em. If you was to ask them, they'd say there's ne'er a seagull in the Midlands, only sparrows. But there they am, the seagulls, up above their heads all the time. OK?'

At last we emerged at the top of the bank and began to walk across the playing fields to the school.

'Don't look so surprised,' Tracy said, after I'd been silent for a while. 'It wasn't my idea about the seagulls. 'Twas me dad's. But it's right enough, you try it. Not on David, though. I shouldn't wonder if he's read somewhere in a book that seagulls do come inland in winter. Try your Valerie.'

'God, no. I certainly won't,' I said.

Tracy laughed madly. I suddenly saw she could look

quite pleasant if she wanted, even though she's such a weirdie.

It was not until dinner time that I got a chance to talk to David, though I'd been looking for one all morning. I wanted to repair the damage done on Black Friday. Of course, there is supposed to be a set list of people on each dining table, but what with some children being absent and different prefects or teachers being on duty, it isn't all that difficult for changes to happen. The noisiest boys and the giggliest girls generally manage to get on to the same table if they want to. I planned to take Kevin Bayliss's place on David's table.

After the grace had been muttered, I looked at the pitiful wreck of a dinner doled out to me by the table monitor and smiled at Dave, who was sitting next to me. I suppose I had no need to feel surprised because he didn't smile back warmly, but I did feel a slight check, all the same.

'Not much to eat on this table,' I commented quietly.

'Lucky to get anything,' the monitor said, having miraculously overheard.

'And where's the meat?' I asked.

'It'll be crawling out of the cauliflower any moment,' he replied.

David said nothing to all this conventional school banter, but looked abstractedly into the distance. Perhaps there was something specially interesting outside the window.

The first-form boy right opposite me suddenly flicked a piece of potato at David, and woke him up.

'Thanks for the extra,' he said. 'But I wish you'd pass it on your spoon instead of flicking it.'

'Want any more?' the little boy asked. 'He's gid me too many taters.'

'No,' David answered coolly. 'A forkful's too much.'

'It's fair shares,' the monitor said. There was a groan

from the regulars, who knew he kept the best for himself. I still didn't know how I'd come to get next to no meat, and turned to David for support again.

'Look. Not worth eating,' I said.

'Perhaps a ghost ate it,' he answered bitterly.

The rest of the table had started to attack the monitor on his weakest point, the current form of Birmingham City, of which he was a blinkered and frenzied supporter. No one heard David's insulting remark, but it was a tense moment, a crisis in the whole of the Abigail quest. I had every right to be wild at him. But I suddenly remembered Tracy and the seagulls. If the boy was ignorant, then I couldn't blame him.

'It wouldn't keep a ghost alive,' I said with an effort. It wasn't a clever rejoinder, and coming after such a wait, it couldn't be called 'quick as a flash' repartee. There wasn't even any lightness in the way I said it. All the same, it worked the miracle.

'Oh, I'm sorry, Teresa,' David said quietly. 'It must have been your friend Val. She's got no time at all for ghosts.'

'I know that,' I replied. 'She was most peculiar on Saturday when I saw her.'

'She told me on Friday she thought *you* were.'

'So I was a bit on Friday. It's partly Val's fault, though. She just mocks everything I say.'

'She was on Friday afternoon. All the way down to Blackheath.'

'And you were with her?'

'Her and Kevin. He was going to buy me an Aztec he owes me, but of course, she had to tag herself on the end.'

'She would! I just wish a ghost'd haunt her, that's all.'

'She kept on about ghosts—finding them funny, I mean. She's got an obsession. But although she kept on laughing at you, I didn't, Teresa. You don't usually make things up entirely.'

'Or if I do,' I admitted, 'I say they're made up. This certainly wasn't, I swear it wasn't.'

At this point we were interrupted by being told to take the dishes back to the serving hatch, and I lost track. But at the end of the dinner, when we'd put the chairs on the tables, ready for the cleaners, David and I walked out together along the corridor. Out of his pocket he took what seemed to be a bag of biscuits.

'Have a biscuit?' he asked.

'No thanks, I've just had dinner.'

'Call that dinner? More like butterfly food, that was.'

'Well, no thanks all the same.'

'Go on, I'd like you to.'

I looked in the bag. There was only one chocolate biscuit ring left, nestling cosily among the crumbs of past biscuits.

'There's only one left,' I protested. 'I couldn't take it from you.'

'But you must. Look, I'll break it in two. That'll be quite fair.'

'Oh, all right. It's generous of you.'

It wasn't so much that I wanted to eat half a chocolate biscuit ring. It was just that it seemed to seal the alliance again.

David broke the ring in two, and we laughed as the crumbs flew everywhere. Then we each munched our half as we struggled along the corridor against the tide of humanity. We smiled and laughed, but couldn't talk. One reason was the biscuit in our mouths, but in any case there was too much noise to shout above it. So we agreed to leave a detailed discussion of the ghost story until four o'clock.

13
The Sampler Smashes

At the four o'clock bell that afternoon we left school as soon as we could. The pale sunlight of the morning had lingered till about three, but the hoar frost had never left the playing fields and mist was hanging about not far off. Perhaps it would close like a blanket over Old Hill, stopping buses and making everyone late home from work. There was a lot to do before anything like this happened. I had decided that if we moved very fast there was time to show David both the sampler and the canal bridge before Mom got home from her part-time job around six.

As we left the back entrance of the school and stumbled down the grass bank, we overtook Tracy. I didn't want a threesome. Still, we slackened our pace, out of politeness.

'Gosh, don't wait for me,' she said, surprised. 'I ain't hurrying tonight.'

'You sure?' I queried. 'Dave and me are in a rush.'

' 'Course. I've got to go to me A'ntie's and she ain't back till five.'

'OK,' said Dave.

'OK,' I said. 'Ta-ta.' And we went on ahead. But afterwards I thought: if she's in no hurry, why was she that quick off the school premises? She beats me at times.

Going across the school field I repeated my story about the ghost. It was a breathless tale, still muddled and unlikely, though this time I told it honestly. It wasn't surprising that he still didn't believe me.

'And yet it's me that doesn't believe in the supernatural,' I sighed.

'It's not that I don't believe in the supernatural, Teresa,' he said. 'But can ghosts be real? I mean, it doesn't make sense.'

'Well, you did say once we could bring the past to life.'

'Yes. But I didn't mean that way. It's you being so imaginative. It's all this Creative Writing.'

I knew it was nothing to do with Creative Writing. Abigail had appeared through her own wish, not mine.

'Look, David. I was terrified. You can't suppose I'd deliberately frighten myself like that. I sometimes think Abigail's taking me over. She's getting to be part of me, somehow ... And I keep on thinking of that wrong verdict.'

'You don't know it was wrong.'

'Yes, I do. There was something said in court which makes me sure, but I can't seem to remember what.'

'Well, coroners aren't usually wrong,' David said firmly.

'There wasn't enough motive, though. I mean, you wouldn't commit suicide just because your father told you not to meet someone. You'd meet them in secret.'

David was very thoughtful. 'These Victorians ...' he finally said. 'They *were* driven to suicide. Ever read *Adam Bede*?'

'Good gracious, no. I've heard of it.'

'Well, in that book, Hetty Sorrell keeps on wanting to drown herself because she's going to have a baby, and she can't marry the father.'

'Fast little whatsit!' I exclaimed, looking away.

'Yes.'

'But not Abigail,' I went on urgently.

'Well then,' he went on. 'If you think David and Abigail went on meeting in secret, we've got to find out where. Any ideas?'

'Dave? You know, I keep finding things out about

Abigail. Don't you think you could find something out about David?'

'Not just by imagination. I'm no creative writer. I can guess things from evidence. I like doing that, but you don't catch me seeing ghosts.'

'What can you guess, then?'

'I tell you what's odd,' he said. 'It's funny he happened to be passing the canal just after she was drowned. Was he going to meet her somewhere down there? Had they got a meeting place by the canal? Somewhere secret?'

'They could have. I wonder if Henry Parkes guessed? He might know his horse whip'd never do the trick. He'd know his daughter'd just defy him, surely?'

'You've always said he didn't believe in the suicide, and that was what came out in the inquest, too.'

'But if he'd made a bigger fuss at the inquest, his daughter would have seemed disobedient, which might have been worse . . . So he made his protest, then arranged secretly for a quiet burial, and had "innocent of all harm" engraved on the headstone.'

'If he *did* have that engraved on. You always said that he didn't, before.'

All this talk had taken us a long way towards home, and the early downstairs lights of our council estate began to show through the crisp winter dusk. It wasn't even half past four by my wristwatch, and the twinkly lights were emerging all the way across to Cradley Heath and Brierley Hill. In the west, the clouds burnt red and yellow, silhouetting the crest of Cawney Hill so that the trees looked like cardboard. We dropped off the road down a steep rough path into the back of the estate. I felt a qualm or two about bringing David into our council house, because I had an idea his life might be much posher, and that he might not like the lingering smell of fish and chips which completed the Chinese Restaurant effect.

The front path was still filthy with workmen's rubbish, but at least the mud had caked hard with last night's frost. I reached the key from under the mat.

'Wipe your feet because of the mud,' I said.

We opened the door and entered the hall, which felt a very daring thing to do. The house seemed twice as silent as usual, brooding and questioning this double intrusion by its own tenant, Teresa Willetts, leading a complete stranger, David Ray. It was almost completely dark with the door shut, and of course it was up to me to switch the lights on. I was hesitant, though, and waited there for several seconds, listening for oddness.

'Is there a light switch?' asked the practical boy.

'Half a tick,' I answered, waking up.

When I switched the light on, I saw at once what disaster had struck now. The sampler had slid from the wall, smashing the glass and pulling out the picture hook.

'That's it, the sampler,' I said. 'On the floor.'

He looked doubtful. I suppose he was wondering whether we usually keep our Victorian antiques on the hall floor.

'Gosh, what a mess! The glass seems to have smashed,' I added helplessly, bending down to pick up the wreckage and restore it. 'It's all over the place.'

'If you're going to pick it up, do be careful. You can't save the glass,' David warned.

I did pick it up, but not carefully, and a splinter of glass gashed my hand. I panicked this time, but he didn't. I felt the sampler a live thing, which twisted out of my hands and fell to the floor again. He saw only dangerous slivers of glass.

'Shove your hand under the tap. Where's the sticking plaster?' he asked.

It wasn't a bad gash, but the bright crimson blood dripped on to our yellow kitchen tiles so that I was reminded again of the colour of gorse, fiery and alive.

'I said, shove your hand under the tap,' David repeated. 'Never mind dreaming about the colour pattern.'

'Pass us that sticking plaster off the shelf,' I said, wondering how on earth he had guessed about the yellow and red. He handed it to me, and within a minute I had put the plaster on. Meanwhile David had brushed all the scattered glass into the dustpan, and the hall looked tidy. What glass was still in the sampler frame he removed, and put the whole lot in the pedal bin.

'A medal for you,' I said. 'Prompt action.'

He looked pleased, and we then went to look at the now harmless sampler, which was coming adrift from its frame.

We found it had been backed on to cardboard, which was yellow with age and grey with dust. David held the sampler up to the light to look at the writing, then turned it round to look at the cardboard backing. As he did so, the card moved away from the sampler cloth, and he carefully put it down on the kitchen table.

'Look. There's been something between the two here. A mark in the card, and a lighter colour. A ring, by the looks of it.'

There was certainly a round indentation in the cardboard.

'A ring?' I was nonplussed.

'It must be. It couldn't be a coin, because you can see both sides of it. But it's gone now; there's no sign of it except the discolouring and this slight indentation. It was a ring, though, there's no doubt.'

I hopped around excitedly, as well I might. Then I felt this was a bit wild, with David there. So I came and looked at the sampler over his shoulder. We held it up very carefully, and looked at it from all sides.

'It's well stitched,' David said. 'The letters are so clear, and the gorse flowers so bright after all this time. It's amazing the yellow hasn't faded.'

'I don't know what they'll say about it breaking,' I commented. 'But, oh! Look at the time!'

I had heard the diesel train's horn as it started from the station down the road. By now the lighted snake of suburban carriages would be crawling purposefully up behind our garden towards the tunnel under High Fields.

'Come on, Dave. We must get a shift on! I want to show you the actual bridge before you go, and you don't want any trouble when you get home.'

'No fear. I don't even want any comment.'

We let ourselves out of the front again, switching the light off and putting the key back under the mat.

'Where did you buy the sampler anyway?' David asked as we closed the front gate.

'I don't know. I suppose it must have come from a junk shop or something. Funny how it's come back almost to the place where it was made.'

We walked through the estate to the other canal bridge, stopping a minute to examine the little brook that emerges from a culvert near to the railway line and twinkles down into the cut. If you shut your eyes, you can think you're by some dancing Welsh mountain stream. Then we went across the bridge to the road.

'This isn't the bridge,' I told him. 'It's the other side of the railway.'

'No. I can see this one just leads to the estate.'

By now it was pitch dark except for the street lights and the cosy room lights in the houses and cottages. Other people's rooms look very inviting when you see them through the windows on a winter evening. But more so when you're by yourself than when you have a friend.

We went under the railway and on to the new Wright's Bridge. From it we gazed at the dark still water. I felt very apprehensive here, because this was the very place where

I'd seen that pale face reflected by the side of my own. David was thoughtful, and said nothing. I mastered my nerves by myself. Then I was able to explain to him how the bridge had changed since Abigail's time, and how the hump-backed brick parapet with its smooth rounded top would have been easier to climb over than this metal and wood structure.

'Yes,' said David. 'But she didn't climb over it.'

'Well, how did she . . . ?'

'I don't quite remember from the report. I simply must look it up in our notes. But I do know it stuck in my mind that she didn't actually jump from the bridge. Now, that's funny, when you come to think of it.'

I wished we had the inquest report with us, but we hadn't. We couldn't for the life of us recall the detail.

Back under the railway bridge we went, and started to climb the hilly road which comes out at the top of Gosty Hill, the road down which David Caddick came on the evening when Abigail drowned. It is still rather countrified at the start, with old cottages on either side, and an old pub called The Boat with a bright sign on it, showing a narrow boat on the canal nearby. The road soon gets mixed up with the estate though, and it starts to look tatty. A little way along, a strange round tower stands by the side of the road, with a domed wire-mesh grille on the open top. It's right beside someone's gate post, sticking out into the footpath.

'Whatever's that?' David asked. 'Some other historical relic?'

'Don't you know?' I asked, surprised. 'It's the canal air vent. Not all that historical.'

I've said it was dark. But it wasn't dark enough to hide you if you needed it. Normally, we wouldn't need it, but all of a sudden we did, because riding along the footpath on a two-wheeler came Wayne Coley, who lives next door but one, is fifteen, and a pest. I knew he wouldn't pass a chance like this.

'Yoo-hoo! Grammar grubs!' he shouted. He ran his cycle into the wall with a bump, slid off, jumped the gate, slung a newspaper in at the porch of the house and jumped back again.

'On me pitch, wor yer?' he asked. 'Last Thursday, I mean. Did Steph's round for her, dai' yer?'

'So what?'

'Yo put the papers through the boxes, dai' yer? Agin th'union rules, tharris. Yo'll ha' the customers all wantin' the same. Chuck 'em on the mat, Teresa Willetts, chuck 'em on the mat.'

'I'm paid to put them through the door, Wayne,' I said, baiting him.

'On the mat. Or I'll clobber yer. And who's the boy-friend?'

'No boy-friend, Wayne, but a sight more friendly than you.'

'I got me round. I cor waste time on yo lot of kids. I'm off.'

So saying, he snatched Dave's cap and hurled it on to the top of the canal air vent, ran his bike over my foot, and was off down the road, whistling and swerving madly from side to side. I almost felt sorry there was no car coming up from Old Hill to knock him down.

'Has your cap gone down the hole?' I asked anxiously.

'No. I can still see it. Look, that lump against the sky.'

Perhaps these canal vents are twelve foot, perhaps only ten. Too tall to reach the top, though. David stood there, downcast, trying to work out some way of poking the cap down with a stick.

'Oh, come here,' I exclaimed. 'You'll never get it down by thinking.' And with that, I climbed up on the wall which stood by the vent. Even so, I could not reach the top.

'Give us a leg up,' I called down. So he, too, climbed on the low brick wall, and helped me scrabble up the side of the tower, clinging on to the metal grille to lever myself up. One hand touched the cap.

There was a pause. I had so rushed the poor lad, he had had no chance to be courteous, as I suppose he'd have liked. As it turned out, this was a good job.

'Teresa,' he called. 'I'm sorry. I should really . . .'

'Shut up a minute,' I told him. 'Down in the canal tunnel, on the towpath. There's something going on. People talking.'

'What? You wouldn't think it'd echo up.'

'It's not an echo. It's the actual sound. The vent leads straight down into the tunnel, they all do. That's why the metal cage is on the top. Folks like young Wayne'd be bound to fall in if they hadn't got them.' My voice had dropped to a harsh whisper.

I looked down and saw David silent and rather tense. His eyes were on my foot, which was in danger of kicking his face; there was no foothold on the tower, and I was keeping my balance by leaning my body on the metal frame and clinging on with one hand.

'What is it?' he asked after a bit. 'What's going on?'

I hardly heard him, so engrossed was I in the words which came eerily out of the dark depths over which I was suspended. I suppose it seemed to him an age before I finally moved my free hand again, stretched out for the cap, and flung it down into the road. At last I descended to the wall beside him, and then jumped to the ground.

'Your weight nearly killed me,' he announced. 'And what if the people had come out of the house while I was perched there waiting to help you down?'

'It's been worth it,' I said. 'We've got more than your cap. Just wait till you hear.' I ignored his edginess, thinking he might still be feeling guilty at not doing the knight errant act, but letting me turn the tables. After all, it was my turn, after the way he'd dealt with the broken sampler.

'What? Whatever were you listening to?'

'Down in the canal. You'll never guess. Our friend David Caddick, talking to . . . well, Abigail, I suppose. It must be.'

'What? Now? That's impossible, Tess; it really is.'

I dusted down my coat. I thought, 'It's the sampler again. It must have worked its magic charm as the glass splintered.'

'Listen,' I said. 'I heard a girl's voice, at first rather vaguely, but calling the other "Dave". She was speaking about a ring, saying "No". She wouldn't take it, didn't want it. "Go on," the chap answered, "I'd like you to"— or something like that, it was. She still hesitated and I heard her say, "I couldn't take it from you," but he told her she must. In the end she took it, I think, and they went away laughing; they sounded very happy.'

'I don't believe it,' he answered. 'I mean, I do believe it, I suppose. But isn't it too much of a coincidence?'

'Well, that's what I heard. Couldn't you hear anything?'

'I might have heard talking,' he said. 'But I didn't know who it was.'

'Well, she called him Dave,' I said.

'It's not that uncommon. And wouldn't a Victorian leave it at David?'

'Maybe,' I replied, not really agreeing. My enthusiasm was wild, and I tried to drag his thoughts and feelings along with me. 'It must have been an echo, lingering from distant time.'

'Really, Tess. You're no physicist. I wouldn't like to chance saying that to our Physics teacher.'

'What else was it, then?'

'Oh, I don't know. Perhaps it was two people now, twentieth-century people who happen to have the same name.'

'Well, we know Abigail had a ring,' I pointed out. 'It was stitched in the sampler. Mercy me! Henry Parkes'd have been furious if he'd known. I suppose that's why she did stitch it in.'

'Those voices could've been anyone,' he said flatly. 'And that's that.' Did I sense slight jealousy on his part, now that I seemed to be getting direct transmissions from 1860?

'Anyone called David,' I answered, standing my ground. 'With someone called Abigail. Planning to give a ring as a token to mark their love.'

By this time we were coming down the road again, and had passed the station. I thought of seeing him on the bus and then going home. Then I remembered the wreck of the sampler, and thought I'd better go home quickly and get the tea to make up. The buses are few and far between. In fact, there's only one bus, which keeps going backwards and forwards all day up and down hill. Very boring for the driver. Still, I somehow didn't want to go back home, and might have been very late, only the bus came into sight in the far distance, and David put a spurt on to catch it, flinging his good-byes over his shoulder. I couldn't resist waiting to see it go by. He'd got his head in his homework book already, and the bus swirled past in a mist of diesel fumes, leaving me alone to face the sampler again.

I had managed to get the tea laid and the bread cut in time, so everyone was happy. They didn't hold the sampler against me, and were inclined to joke about its downfall.

'I don't know why we keep the old thing,' Jean said.

'It's quite nice,' I said cautiously.

'Oh, we all know you. You're saft about it.'

'Bit of your mom's old rubbage,' Dad put in. 'Worth a bob or two, I suppose.' That probably meant he thought it was worth a lot. I don't know if it is.

'It wouldn't be rubbage, as you call it, to the one as

stitched all those flowers on it. I wonder she could see against she'd finished all that close work,' Mom said.

'Where did it come from, anyway?' I asked. I didn't want them to look too closely at the stitching. The fact was, the breaking glass had gashed the sampler, and I was going to have to add my clumsy stitches to Abigail's fine ones to repair it. I had no doubt that I should be the one to repair it, and felt dimly that it was my fault it had fallen down.

'I can't say for sure. Why don't you ask Nanny when we go to Weston? We'll be going on Saturday, all being well.'

'Should she know?' I asked, rather surprised.

'If anyone does. That sampler was hanging in our dining-room—if that's what you'd call it—at home. She may have got it from that old junk shop in High Street. She was always there. I don't know really.'

'You still haven't told us how it came to fall down,' said Jean.

'I don't know. When I got in, there it was on the floor. The hook was right out of the wall. Looked as though it'd thrown itself off.'

'Time it was reframed,' said Dad. 'It looks a bit frowsty.'

'I'm going to clean it tonight after I've got my homework done.'

'If yo ask me, they give yo too much homework.' Dad can never understand about Education. 'And be careful yo don't wear your eyes out sewing.'

'It's all right, Dad. We have to do the homework. And I'll enjoy the sewing.' This was a piece of bravado, because I don't really care for handicraft all that much. The sampler took some sewing, and caused a few more drops of blood on my hands. But I stitched away carefully, and for me it was good sewing.

Later I tried my finger against the ring mark. It was too big. This didn't really surprise me, though I thought: I bet it would have fitted Jean.

Our deductions seemed to make sense to me. Abigail had been given the ring by her lover, but hadn't been able to wear it, so had stitched it into the sampler for safety. In this place, between the sampler and its frame, it went very well with the text on the front: *WHERE YOUR TREASURE IS, THERE SHALL YOUR HEART BE ALSO*. That ring was Abigail's treasure, all right.

14
A Plan of Fiery Holes

The following Thursday was December 1st, and a light
flurry of snow reminded us of the season. It was a fortnight
now since that meeting of the local history club had sent us
creeping round the shadowy churchyard. Our teacher had
asked David and myself to talk about our discoveries. I
wasn't too happy about this; but still, we had come armed
with the sampler (no glass in the frame) and David was
going to do most of the talking. We should have brought the
death certificate as well, but of course, I'd ripped that to
shreds, then burnt it. I never told David about this, and I
hoped he'd forgive me when he knew.

'Seen one of them before,' Kevin called out, as the
sampler was brought out of its brown paper wrapping.
'Tracy brought one last time.'

'The sampler, you mean?' I asked.

' 'Course,' he answered, sucking the last of a troach drop.
'All little stitches and flowers. What flowers am they,
anyway?'

'Can't you tell by the spiky bits?' David asked. 'Gorse,
it is.'

'Tracy had glass in hers. Yourn looks a bit tatty to me.'

'Fair's fair, Kev,' Tracy barged in. 'We can't all afford
to keep our heirlooms in good nick.'

'It's not really an heirloom, I must admit,' I told them.
'My nanny had it off a junk stall.'

Kevin would talk the hind leg off a donkey. He's cheeky
with it, and I was glad when our teacher told him to let us

get on in peace. We told them all about the gravestone, the *Innocent of all harm* and the parish register. I read pieces out of our copy of the inquest. No one seemed very interested, and I didn't dare to bring in the disreputable ghost.

'You've been properly stirring the ghosts up,' said Mr Reed, speaking truer than he thought. 'Do you think there can be much more to find out?'

'I still can't settle the suicide,' I replied. 'I can't work out exactly what did happen.'

'Teresa's sure she didn't do it,' David put in. 'And that's the reason for the odd words on the inscription.'

'Any other clues from the papers of the week?' Mr Reed asked.

'We only spent the one evening down there,' David answered.

'I couldn't do with another session in there,' I said hastily. 'You hardly dare breathe.'

'Well, you're in luck. I'll be going into the library on Saturday. I'll have a look for you if you like. I always enjoy old papers.' Mr Reed's eyes glinted at the prospect of the chase.

'Was that your garden fell into the pit shaft, Teresa?' asked Tracy Dobbs. 'You never said.'

'How do you know?'

'*County Express*, Friday. Mr Thomas Willetts; that's your dad, ain't it? Said it was once the Fiery Holes mine. Was it a mess?'

'You bet,' I said. 'Still is. Mud everywhere.'

'I've got a map of it, then, if it is Fiery Holes.'

'Eh?' David started forward, excited.

'A map; an old plan. I've got it in me sack. I thought I'd bring it in, in case you'd be interested, being as it's your cabbages.'

Mr Reed looked as interested as I felt, and David peered

over the top of his glasses as if afraid to trust them. How ever did Tracy keep turning up these old things? She seemed a bit of a mine herself.

'Here,' she said. 'Catch 'old. Go on, it won't bite you.' And she produced from her satchel a faded roll, done up with pink ribbon. There was scrawly writing on the back, of the kind I could now recognise as copperplate.

Mr Reed took charge, and laid the plan on the desk top. He unrolled it carefully, while I watched for signs of it crumbling away. It did not do so, however. True, there was a patch of pinkish damp, and the margin was torn. But it was easily legible, and quite strong.

'Look,' Tracy showed us. 'Fiery Holes mine. All crossed out, and writin' on it. Mind, I can't quite read the writin'. It's for you to look at, Teresa, if you've a mind. Watch out, you other cheeky devils! It's her garden as has fallen in, not yourn.'

'Well, I hope you'll let me look at it too, Tracy,' Mr Reed asked mildly.

'Yes, Mr Reed. Sorry, sir. Only it's her garden, so I thought she should be first.'

The map was dated in the 1850s, and seemed to be a plan of coal mines surveyed by one Alfred Chandler of Cradley Heath. Pencil alterations had been made over the top, and it seemed as though when a mine was closed, this was noted on the plan. Near to Slack Hillock, the words *Fiery Holes* had been run through in pencil, and a date put on, similar to the other dates on the plan. The date was December 8th '60, and there was a word by it which I couldn't make out.

Mr Reed looked excitedly over my shoulder. It was taking all his self control not to snatch the map from me. All the others were pushing me too, so it was no wonder I couldn't steady the plan to read it.

'What's that say?' I had to admit myself beaten.

'Let's look,' said the teacher, satisfied at last. 'Wildfire,' he proclaimed. 'Wildfire. That's why it was shut. Wildfire. That's when the coal and slack at the bottom of the pit flare up, and you can't stop it when it's once started.'

'8th December is two days before Abigail's death,' David pointed out.

'Funny,' said Kevin, who had no idea what we were talking about.

As for me, I saw startling light. But was it good, wholesome rays, or devil's fiery light, malevolent and scorching?

'Does that help with your Abigail hunt?' Tracy asked. She had seen the point, I felt sure. Fiery Holes, the mine where David Caddick had worked, was closed the same week as Abigail's death, only two days before it. I could see a possible connection, all right.

'It might do,' David said, more cautiously.

'Me dad found it,' Tracy said proudly. 'In a heap of rubbish down the solicitor's where he works. Handyman at these offices in Halesowen. It don't matter what it is, if it's old, me dad'll have it. The whole room over the entry's full of stuff. Dad, he loves old things.'

'Well, thanks for bringing it, Tracy,' I said. 'In fact, it was your sampler that started us off in the first place.'

'You'm welcome. As long as you don't kill yourselves.'

'We're not likely to,' David said, with a polite smile. He never takes Tracy seriously.

'Messin' about with the dead you easily might. And canals. It's the honest Gospel truth that's what happened me elder brother Joe. He'd a' been seventeen last August. Fell in; only three he was. I never knew him.'

'Tracy, you are gloomy,' I said.

'Not really. I wisht I'd a' met him, that's all. It's funny havin' a brother you han't met. Mom says he's an angel, of course. Her don't say I'm one.'

After the meeting, David and I walked along with Tracy.

8

I was glad, because I thought he ought not to be so uppity with her. I remembered what she'd said on Monday, and how she'd been right about the seagulls (which I'd tested out on three girls later in the week). She's got a perky kind of face, and is very thin. You can cut her accent with a knife, but she doesn't care.

'Our dad's funny,' she said. 'Ain't got two ha'pennies to rub together. But do you know, he never works overtime? All his spare time, he's either doing up old furniture or else down the Army.' (By this she meant the Salvation Army, our local hot-gospellers.) 'Shall you stand that from your husband, Teresa? I shan't.'

I laughed heartily. 'Hadn't thought to have one,' I said.

'You'll be lucky,' she threw back at me. 'It'll be a long time before women's lib comes to our town. If it ever does. Don't know as I want it to.'

We paused to open the swing doors at the front of the school.

'Mind, our dad's got a right. He works hard for hisself in the week, so of course the Lord gets the Sabbath. I wisht he'd sometimes cook the dinner, though, instead of me. Mom's bad in bed, you see.'

'Well, I'd think more of your dad,' I joined in, 'if he did stop at home. He ought to do the dinner, instead of playing the cornet.'

She rounded on me sharply. 'He does it for the Lord,' she said. 'I thought you went to the Wesleyan.'

'I've given up,' I said. David said nothing.

'Shame on you! You want to look out for your soul, you do!'

It was on the tip of my tongue to say I hadn't got one. But a lot of water had flowed under bridges during the last couple of weeks, and I didn't honestly feel sure. I still don't feel sure now; there's been no great conversion. Even if I were to be converted, I don't know what it'd be to. One ghost and a couple of angels don't make a religion. Though, even if it sounds corny, I sometimes do think there must be a weaver to weave the sampler I got involved in. Perhaps one day I'll emerge from all the muddle, and see the patterns plainly. Perhaps we all will. Meanwhile, I just have to envy such people as David and Tracy.

15

Old Photographs

Our Weston trip on Saturday went well. It brought me a tremendous surprise, which I'd never for a minute expected. The weather was cold, but there was no rain or snow, and Dad seemed to enjoy the driving. Jean didn't come; she had her own fish to fry.

I don't quite like Weston out of season. You keep on remembering summer happiness, which you can't indulge in when the sleet is stinging you and the darkness closes in at half past four. But it's always worth visiting Nan, who puts the red carpet down and makes a fuss. There is no washing-up, either, because there are enough grown-ups to do it.

As soon as we got there, I was given some money for sweets. I didn't dawdle along the front; it was too miserable a sight. When I had my sweets, I rushed back to the tall stone house where Nanny has a flat, and leapt up the steep flight of steps. I pushed open the door gingerly; there are pink and blue panes in the door which always rattle, and I'm afraid this coloured glass will fall out one day and disintegrate on the stone floor. Half-way down the narrow, tiled hall, I stopped. Lucky I hadn't made much noise with the front door. Voices could be heard in Nan's back kitchen: Mom and Nan were exchanging news.

News about me, I wondered? Yes, gossip.

'. . . seems to spend half her time doing homework and the other chasing up history from the past.'

'They get restless, don't they, staying on at school?'

'She's got an idea of doing a paper round. Really, I'm not keen, Mother. You don't know what they get up to. It's so early to have to go out in the morning.'

It occurred to me there wasn't much difference between fighting Wayne Coley when I hadn't got a paper round and fighting him if I had. Except I'd be paid for it if I had.

'I wouldn't let her, Lil. I wouldn't really. You can't be too careful.'

'Oh, by the way. She seems to be getting attached to that old bit of embroidery you had from the junk shop. You know, in the hall. I think I'm going to give it her to hang in her bedroom.'

As I listened, I began to have a conscience about eavesdropping, but I couldn't move a muscle.

'What's that, dear? D'you mean the sampler?'

'Yes. That's it.'

'Oh, no, Lily. That wasn't from a junk shop, though it may look like it.'

'I've always thought it was. I told Teresa so.'

I coughed loudly, and opened the kitchen door wide so that I could get in and confront them.

'Hullo, love,' said Nan. 'You OK for sweets now?'

'Yes, thanks,' I answered. 'It's very kind of you. Excuse me asking, but did I just hear you say the sampler wasn't from a junk shop?'

'It was not,' said Nan, 'though it might look like it. It may not be any oil painting, but an aunt of mine did it, years before I was born. You want to look at it careful some time, Teresa. You'll see it's got a lot of work in it. Mind, I wouldn't want it here. I've seen enough of old-fashioned things in my lifetime. But it is old; must be above a hundred years.'

'1854,' I said. 'Or at least, that's the date on it. But perhaps that's wrong too, if the name's wrong.'

The world of Abigail seemed to bubble and fade away

from me. Somehow I couldn't square the beautiful sorrowing girl of seventeen, or her eleven-year-old counterpart that had stitched so diligently, with a picture of my grandmother's aunt. It was incredible: I saw the person who stitched the sampler now as an old, old woman.

'Oh, I don't think the name's wrong.' Nan was getting out the cups for some coffee.

'I had no idea,' said Mom. 'I thought you'd have bought it from that old junk shop in High Street.'

'Not me. It was useful things I bought at the junk shop. I had some bargains too: chairs, tables, all sorts. But not that thing. I'd never have kept it, only my grandad gave it me. He told me he specially wanted me to keep it. I suppose it might be worth something by now.'

I was quite bewildered, a long way from sorting all this out into common sense.

'It was worth something then,' I flashed out. 'But where did your grandad get it?'

'I've told you. My aunt made it. Sewed it herself. Little girls used to do that sort of thing in them days. They never soiled their hands with real work. My family were gentlefolk, you know.'

I was speechless.

Mom laughed. 'I know we're not that now, anyway. But I have heard great-grandad had a lot of money.'

'A fool and his money are soon parted,' Nan said sagely. 'But, do you know, standing here's not doing much good to my arthritis. It's all right coming to the seaside for your lungs, but it plays havoc with your rheumatism.'

'But please!' I begged. 'Please! Tell me the rest of the story. You can't just leave it in the middle.'

'Oh, bother,' Nan exclaimed. 'Now look at that! With us canting and cag-magging, the milk's boiled over.'

'Well, will you faithfully promise to tell me everything?' I demanded, very worked up. 'I simply must know.'

'There's nothing to tell,' Nan replied, mopping up the scalding milk with a dish cloth. I could see Mom eyeing me apprehensively. She obviously thought I was getting over-excited, or some such imaginary grown-up thing. I heeded the danger signal.

'Oh, it doesn't matter,' I heard myself lying. 'Perhaps this afternoon.'

'Well, I don't mind talking about old times,' said Nanny. 'Not that they were easy, Teresa. You don't know how lucky you are these days—free schools, cheap housing . . .'

'Oh, no. You're wrong there, Mother. No one could call council houses cheap these days,' Mom objected.

'But at least you know where your next meal's coming from. My mother didn't always. And she was very proud; she'd never borrow. As for the welfare state, she'd have had a blue fit.'

A new bottle of milk was opened, and this time the coffee got made instead of spilt. I decided reluctantly to leave them at it in the kitchen and go into the front room where Dad was listening to the pre-lunch sports programme in case there were any last-minute team changes.

In the afternoon, Dad waited in just long enough to see if Albion would be on the telly this week. When they weren't, he went off out. In the meantime I waited impatiently for Nan to come in from her rest, which she has every afternoon without fail. It was ages before she came. Mom had gone up to a neighbour's flat, and I had nothing to do. There were no books in the room except a few Bible commentaries and a photograph album or two. I sat in the old-fashioned chair, a dull fawn colour, and picked one of these out.

In the album there were faded brown photos of chara-bancs and gusty promenades, groups of forgotten faces, a strange town. I saw Mom at an early age, looking like

Jean, and Nan at an early age, looking like Mom. As I turned back, Nan got younger, till she too looked like Jean, even like me a bit.

There were some red-brown portrait photos right at the front. They showed the main members of the family alive at the end of Victoria's reign. Jean appeared again; and—Good heavens! the ghostly Abigail stared out of a picture labelled *Sarah Parkes*. Next to her, an old gentleman with side whiskers, a great white beard, and a top hat, smiled broadly at me. It hardly surprised me at all, by now, when I turned the photo over and read in faint pencil, *Henry Parkes*. Here was the old colliery owner himself, pictured in our Nan's photograph album!

A minute afterwards, Nanny came into the room. She sat down on the settee, drew me across to sit beside her, and took her glasses from their case. Putting them on, she wrinkled up her nose and took the photo from me.

'Oh, yes,' she said. 'That's my grandad Parkes. He was a bit of a one. He owned coal mines, you know. Before the floods swept the lot. There was a little back on insurance, but not much ... That's my Auntie Sarah. Doesn't she look like you? Exactly the same mouth, you've got. And you've got her eyes, too.'

'Nanny, please could you tell me about your aunt that did the embroidery? Do you know anything about her?'

Nan settled herself deep into the cushions.

'Yes,' she began. 'A bit. Not that I met her, of course. She'd be a step-aunt, I think, really. Or a half-aunt. She died years before I was born. They say she was a very wilful girl and got engaged to marry an ordinary collier. In those days, people were very careful not to get mixed up with their inferiors, and I believe they didn't like this engagement at all. Though, of course, after the pits were all flooded and the capital went, it all showed how wrong they'd been. That side of the family were snobbish.'

'They must have been,' I agreed, praying silently that she'd know more and go on.

'My own dad was only a collier. So the Parkes family had to come to it in the end.'

'Nan, do you know any more about the half-aunt? How she died?'

'Not for sure. You see, it was thirty years before I was born. And my old grandad Parkes had married again. They used to tell me his first wife had died through the shock of losing her only daughter so young. Anyway, he married my Gran, lucky for us.'

'But haven't you heard anything about the girl's death?' I persisted.

'Mmm. As a matter of fact, Grandad Parkes had quite a complex about it. He never had any faith in lawyers after that. That's why he didn't fight the insurance people over the mine flooding. If he had, we might all be rich.'

This sounded very much like wishful thinking, or an old wives' tale. But if Henry Parkes was always cross with lawyers, that fitted in with the inquest report, and my theory that he rejected the verdict.

Nanny stole my thoughts. 'The verdict on her death was suicide, I believe. But he never could credit that his daughter would do such a thing in her right mind. Not that she wouldn't kill herself, exactly; but that she wouldn't kill herself over a collier. If it had been a prince, he'd have believed it. She drowned in a canal; at Dudley, was it?'

I didn't dare to correct her, in case she stopped talking.

'You know, he was really dotty. It preyed on his mind ever after. He kept trying to find any friends of his daughter to talk about it. The only one who seemed to comfort him was the maid, who'd been in the house when the girl was alive. Maria was it? I don't remember . . .'

'Susanna,' I prompted.

'Well, that's right. So it was. It was Susanna. However did you know?'

'I don't know really. Not for sure. I keep trying to piece bits together. I know about this Susanna Caddick.'

'My grandad seemed to get to rely on her. I suppose she was his only link with his dead daughter. He used to go over to Netherton where she lived to his dying day. Funny chap she married, with a peg-leg, named John Roper. They used to call him Dot and Carry One John. I knew them both. In those days, everyone knew everyone else.'

'You see,' I said, twisting a piece of my hair round and round my finger. 'I don't think your aunt killed herself either. I just don't know what happened. And I don't think I'll ever actually prove it. But I'm determined to know for myself. She means me to know,' I added, my voice trailing off.

'How can you, you strange girl? What's past's done with.'

'I know exactly where it happened. I've got to know the spot very well.'

'Now be careful, Teresa, with canals. They're treacherous. You can swim, I suppose?'

'No. But I'm not going to fall in myself. I promise.'

'You don't know what you'll fall into. You must leave that to Providence.'

But, I thought, if there was Providence, how does she know Providence doesn't want me to find out about Abigail? I might be destined to find out.

Now that I knew Abigail had been a relation, I realised that I wasn't suprised. All the time I had been tracking down her story, I had felt her in some way part of myself, sharing my own failings and virtues, if I've got any, and almost directing me. Still, I was glad to know what the connection was: a tie of blood, which resulted in a similar cast of mind, similar feelings, even a faint physical resemblance.

16

Jean's New Ring

We were late back from Weston that night, though Dad drove back up the motorway as fast as he could. I felt the air get friendlier as we neared the Black Country, and when I saw the yellow lights appear, which turn M5 into an 'urban motorway', I felt content. Even Mom said 'Home again', with a sigh, when she scrambled out of the car. And she calls Old Hill 'this dump'.

My foot had gone to sleep, and it was past eleven. The front room lights were on, so I knew Jean was in there with Steve. I hoped they'd made up their difference of opinion by now, whatever it had been about.

On went the concealed lighting. The blank space where the sampler usually hung stared at me, and I could hear the faint noise of the telly turned down low. Too late for 'Match of the Day', I thought. Steve opened the front room door.

'Hullo, all,' he said. 'Thought you'd all gone off to sea, washed away or something.'

'No fear,' said Dad. 'Had to drive a bit carefully coming back. Lots of fools there are about, round closing time. The breathalyser ain't med much difference.'

Mom had gone into the front room to see Jean without taking her coat off. She came back excited. 'Do look everyone!' she cried. 'Come here!'

'What at?' Dad asked. 'What's up now?'

'Look. Our Jean's engaged! And what a lovely ring! A bit different, that is. A bit unusual.'

We all rushed into the front room, eager to see the ring on Jean's finger.

'What's that for?' Dad asked. 'I thought it was going to be at Christmas.'

'It nearly didn't happen at all,' said Jean. 'But it has. So all's well that ends well.'

I thought she looked very pretty and happy, her dark blue eyes almost melting away into her head and her face somehow polished, as if she'd had the furniture wax on it.

'Well, love,' said Mom. 'I hope you'll be very happy. We're ever so fond of Steve anyway.'

'Thank you,' said Steve modestly. And what Mom said was true. We are all fond of Steve. As I said, although he's very clever, he doesn't make you feel it at all. You never feel daft with him.

'I'm ever so pleased,' I said, smiling at both of them.

'Well, I'll just get a cup of tea,' Mom decided, 'and take me coat off. Then you can tell us all about it, and we can have a good look at the ring. It is a lovely one, I can see that.'

I sat down, slightly uneasy, on the edge of a chair. It's a new experience when you become a potential sister-in-law. And perhaps aunt (my thoughts ran on) in a few years. Aunt Teresa? Aunt Tess? I tried the words over in my mind.

'Want to see the ring?' Jean asked.

I looked at it. It was very delicate, and had a pattern engraved on it. Instead of having one large stone, it had five smaller ones. They sparkled beautifully.

'It's old, of course,' Jean said proudly. 'An antique. And it hasn't half got a funny story to it. There's only one ring like it.'

'Oh, what happened then?' I asked, flopping over on to the settee with the pair of them.

'It's a long story, Teresa,' said Steve.

'I'd still like to know, though.'

'Well, as your dad said, we were going to wait till Christmas. But the *County Express* gets a bit crowded around then, so we thought we'd bring it forward. Don't tell your mom yet, but we'd like to get married about April.'

'*You* would, you mean,' Jean said with mock indignation.

'Well, anyway. We'd decided to bring it forward. Then I saw this ring, you see, so that decided it.'

'Oh, do get on with the story.' Jean pushed him in the ribs with her elbow.

'I'm trying to if you'll stop pushing me around.'

'There'll be plenty of pushing yet, my lad,' she answered.

'Well, it was last Tuesday,' he went on, ignoring the last remark. 'I was walking along the canal by Waterfall, trying to get together some material for a local studies project. You know the dredger's been working all along from the tunnel mouth to Waterfall Bridge? So, of course, being a nosy parker, and looking for ideas for my project, I thought I'd have a word with the dredgermen. Old boatmen, they were, with a good many years on the canal behind them.

'We started to talk about the rubbish you get in the cut, and how people will chuck bedsteads and old bicycles in. It makes me see red, I can tell you, and these chaps thought so too. But they said they sometimes had a surprise.'

Daylight was beginning to dawn on me. The old ring Jean was so proudly wearing, shiny and glistening as it was, had come out of the canal with a load of mud from the weed-choked bottom.

'That's right,' Steve agreed when I suggested this. 'Covered in mud, they say it was. But gold never tarnishes, and the men spotted it as soon as it came up.'

'It might be any old thing,' Dad said, a bit disgusted, unlacing his shoes.

'No. Because gold's hallmarked, you see,' Steve said. 'See the anchor? The Birmingham hallmark, that is.'

Jean stretched out her hand, and I inspected the hallmark.

'And the letter L, in that kind of writing, tells you the year,' Steve went on.

'So do you mean this ring's the one the dredger brought up? These canal people could be fooling you, you know.'

'Wait a minute, young Teresa. They can't be fooling me. I know it's genuine because I had it valued before I bought it. And I don't see why they should spin this yarn about the canal if it didn't come from there. I don't see why they'd bother lying. I had to persuade them to sell it me, not the other way round.'

Mom returned with the tea.

'Do you know that ring's out of the cut?' I asked, marvelling at its romantic story.

'What? Out of the cut? Oh, dash! Now I've spilt the tea. Stephen! You're never going to give our Jean a ring out of the canal! How d'you mean, out of the canal?'

'It was found by the dredgermen. It's really old,' said Jean, excited.

'Found! I should think you could have gone to the trouble to get a bus into Dudley and buy a new one,' said Mom. She was cross, she really was.

'I paid for it, of course,' Stephen explained, flummoxed by her anger. 'It's better than a new one. It's got a history, it's unique.'

'What? Trash out of the canal for our Jean? Young man, I don't think you realise what a good girl you've got in her. Plenty of girls I know'd have thrown the ring back at you, mud and all. And I don't blame them.'

'Look, Mom,' I interrupted, to make peace. 'When you first saw it, about a quarter of an hour ago, you said how lovely it was. You said it was a bit unusual. Well, it is.

It's a lovely ring. You couldn't buy them like that nowadays.'

'I know. But out of the canal! Really!'

'Oh, Mom,' said Jean. 'I'm happy, so what's the bother? You can see it's a lovely ring. It's got a history behind it. Ever so old, it is. And Steve would've had to pay twice as much in a shop.'

This nearly set Mom off again, as she was sure rings on the cheap were a sign of faint love.

In the meantime, I had been thinking about this ring and wondering. I looked at it on Jean's hand, and thought of the photos I'd seen that day, in which Jean's face had reappeared in this or that ancestor, right back, probably to Abigail Parkes. Jean sat there with the ring flashing in the electric light. Was there any chance that the face and the ring were reunited? Coincidence, or Abigail, could have been taking a hand again. I pulled Steve's sleeve, and demanded to know where exactly the ring had been found.

'Right below Wright's Bridge, they said. You know, that's the bridge that leads on to Station Road from the Sportsman.'

'Yes,' I said in a whisper which tried to conceal my excitement. 'I know the one you mean.'

I went slowly over the next question, in case it ruined everything.

'Did you say you can tell the year from the hallmark?'

'Yes. It's in *Whittaker's Almanack*.'

'What year . . . ?' my voice trailed off.

'1860 it was hallmarked. Right close by in Birmingham, according to the book. That's why it's got an anchor on.'

I knew it would be 1860. There was no surprise at all. Yet one more piece of Abigail's life story now fitted into place.

17
Baptised by a Witch

I was dying to tell David all my discoveries of the weekend. But on Monday morning he was rather late arriving, and I could only manage to talk to him for half a minute on the way down the stairs to assembly. No one can say anything sensible in half a minute.

But I was very surprised when in the first period old Tracy flicked a note across the gangway from her desk to mine. *Please pass to Teresa Willetts*, it said on the front. Inside it read:

Important disclosure of a circular nature, relevant to deceased. When do you want to hear? David.

'Now,' I thought. 'But I can't. Whatever is he on about?'

I wrote underneath: *Library after first sitting if fine. If wet, ruined cottage at T.G.*

If it was fine, I knew the library would be deserted, and we could swop news in peace. If it was wet, which looked likely, we should be surrounded by a chattering throng of people and there'd be no privacy. The ruined cottage would be a better bet, though the next door cottage was occupied by an old witch with a mighty disgusting flow of language, who was just as likely to hurl bricks as insults.

As I guessed, it turned out wet. I took my bright yellow umbrella to guard me, and stepped smartly along the lane to Tippity Green, a desolate area, full of mud and brick ends, threatened on either side by the roadstone quarries with their terrible depths and their spoil banks of yellow-brown. I got into the cottage from the opposite side, so that the witch would not see me, and I was soon perching on some rubble in the remains of the front room. It had crumbled away, and had laths hanging from the ceiling, some red flowery wallpaper still partly attached to the walls, and a wrought-iron fireplace. I shook my umbrella dry and waited impatiently while the rain deluged down. To tell the truth, it was very lonely there, and I didn't want to look too closely at my surroundings. No ghosts, but lots of fag-ends, slugs, bus tickets, all sorts.

At last David arrived, his glasses completely covered with rain water and rain dripping from his hair all round his silly cap. He looked quite ridiculous, and, as usual just recently, it made me feel sorry for him and pleased to be with him all at once.

'Hullo,' he said cheerfully, climbing into the room through the rotting window frame.

'Hullo. Cats and dogs aren't in it,' I said.

'Only the witch's cat, and she should be indoors on a day like this. Every time I meet you it rains.'

'Almost every time, yes. Must mean something.'

'It means the English climate's hopeless,' he answered.

'Well, it's blinking miserable here, mouldering away waiting,' I said with some faint reproach in my voice.

'If I had my violin,' he replied, drying his glasses on a mixture of string and paper handkerchiefs which he'd taken out of his pocket, 'I could play Handel's Water Music to cheer us up.'

I remembered then that he plays the violin in the school orchestra.

'It wouldn't cheer me up. I want to know about this circular news, or whatever it is. Besides, I've got things to tell you, too.'

'Well, listen to this for a story,' he said, ever so keen, hopping from one leg to another. 'When you were away on Saturday . . .'

'How did you know I was going away?'

'You told me on Friday you were going to Weston-super-Mare to see a granny or someone.'

'It turned out to be a granny *and* someone—several people, in fact.'

'Well, anyway. I just happened to go down to the canal where they're dredging at the back of the industrial estate.'

This was a bit off his beat; I wondered what he was doing there.

'The dredger wasn't working on Saturday, so I had a good look at it. It's a super machine, really. It'd bring anything up in the course of time. I wanted to know how wide it was, and whether it was an old narrow boat converted. It'd have to be narrow to go through the locks.

'There didn't seem to be anyone about, so I got on board. But before I could get off again, there was a shout along the towpath and this chap came in sight, taking his dog for a walk. He looked fairly tough, but I had to face him, because I was trapped in the boat, and knew he'd seen me. He bellowed at me again, and the dog gave an unfriendly yowl.

'Well, apparently he thought I was his lad, who'd been messing about on the dredger before. So I thought I'd better apologise, which I did.'

By this time I was on my feet, guessing what David was going to say next. I tried to interrupt, but you might as well try to stop a bus when you're not at a bus stop.

'We got talking about canals and the odd things dredgers bring up sometimes. Lots of things come up, this man said, that don't get into British Waterways' hands. You'll never guess what they found a week or so ago, or where . . .'

'I will, you know. Both,' I finally managed to say. 'Where? By Wright's Bridge, of course. What? Abigail's ring. I bet I'm right.'

He looked at me as if I was the witch next door. How could I possibly have guessed?

'Do you realise, Dave, I was going to tell you that?'

'Not another dream?' he asked.

'No fear,' I answered. 'Our Jean's got the ring as an engagement ring, that's all.' And I told him the news from last Saturday night.

'. . . but would it be Abigail's after all this time?' I asked, as I finished my story.

'Well, it's certainly a queer coincidence, especially Stephen buying it. But it fits in with what's going on around here.'

'What is?'

'I don't know. You tell me.'

'Well, I can't. And we've been through it all before. I do think it's Abigail's ring, though.'

'Yes. I felt certain it was, even before you told me. I'll bet she was often by the canal side.'

'And by the way, I wish you'd put those specs back on,' I told him. 'Surely they're dry by now? You'll rub the glass out of them.'

'I forgot.'

'Well, put them on, for God's sake. You'll drop them and smash them, or something. By the way, I never told you what your vicar said last week did I?' I went on. 'He's got some idea in his mind, I think. Anyhow, he doesn't think it's impossible that she might be still acting on us.'

'Yes. He told me we ought not to give it up. We ought to find out what was needed. But it's never real religion, surely?'

'I wouldn't know,' I answered. 'To me, it seems more real than some things they call religion. But you're the expert.'

'I only listen to what I'm told, and try to works things out sensibly.'

'Well, the things I'm told often make no sense,' I

answered, rather heatedly. 'It's the things I think and feel which seem real ... And that reminds me. The other thing about Saturday just proves my point.'

At last he put his glasses on again, and stared at me with owl-like eyes.

'You know how I've felt about Abigail for weeks? Well, on Saturday, I found out she was my half-aunt,' I said impressively.

'Half-aunt? What's a half-aunt?' he laughed excitedly. 'She certainly sometimes acts as if she's half here and half there, like the Cheshire cat in *Alice*. But, half-aunt! Really, Teresa, you can't have a half-aunt!'

'Look, I'm telling you. I'm related to Abigail. I don't just feel as if I know her, I've actually got the same blood in my veins.'

'Not by now, I shouldn't think,' he said, with a hoot of laughter.

'Oh, very clever. I don't mean literally, you saft nit. You know perfectly well what I mean.'

'I do. I'm sorry,' he said humbly.

'So when I sort of glimmered she was taking me over, it was true. In a way we are connected, and can't help it. Despite the time passing.'

'Mmm. It might explain why she looked like you, as you said she did.'

'Oh, she must have. You should have seen those photos. Generation after generation my Nanny has in her album, all looking like Jean. And perhaps Jean does look like me sometimes. The same eyes.'

He gave an unexpected sigh and kicked a brick end, wallop, against the old fireplace. A trickle of decomposed plaster spilled out on to the floorboards.

'I wish I had your imagination. Life must be much more exciting.'

'I don't know about that. And I don't "imagine" on

purpose. And anyway, when you say "imagine" it sounds
not real. But, David, you must know it is real to me. I don't
care if anyone else says it isn't, but surely you must know
it's real?'

'Honestly, Tess. I didn't mean to say it wasn't.' He
looked taken aback by my fierceness. 'Of course I believe
you, even if no one else does. Oh gosh,' he broke off. 'Just
look at the time! We've gone and done it again. Five
minutes to the bell.'

We began to climb back over the broken window-sill,
on to the mossy garden path. While we had been talking,
the trickle of plaster had continued at the top of the
fireplace, and a sudden thump announced that a loose brick
had fallen.

'My umbrella,' I suddenly shouted. 'It's still pouring,
and that's my only protection! I've left it in the room.'

I scrambled over the sill again, while David hung about
rather nervously outside. But the bump in the decaying
fireplace had roused the witch. As I climbed through the
window space once again, after retrieving my umbrella,
the flaking door of the neighbouring cottage opened and she
hobbled on to the step, not three yards from where I was
jumping off the ledge.

'I'll drown yer!' she shouted, and began to pour out vile
abuse which I can't repeat. I thought she must mean drown
in a torrent of dark curses, but as I slithered down the blue
brick steps to the road a bucketful of water hurtled through
the air after me. Dave was rather ungallantly first in the
flight, and waited panting outside the stumpy gates. He
didn't catch any of the bucket's contents. As for me, I was
lucky too. I only received a baptism of splashes across my
forehead, when I could have been a drowned rat. But the
sky was still tipping it down from the clouds as black as
judgement day. I put up my umbrella, and like two
conspirators we hurried back to our lessons.

18

What Happened to Abigail Parkes?

I thought I'd got away from the witch without any harm coming to me, but as it turned out, I hadn't. Just as I walked up the path to our front door about a quarter to five, I sneezed. I went on sneezing for about five minutes, and when Mom came out of the kitchen I must have looked a thorough weirdie: dripping umbrella, wet feet, red nose —they all added up to trouble.

'You can just change your clothes at once, Teresa,' she said. 'I haven't got time to nurse you in bed . . .'

But she had to have a couple of days off all the same, I'm sorry to say. During the evening, I kept sneezing more and more, and the homework began to look grey and misty in front of my eyes. I managed to finish it, but, oh dear, was Mom cross about it!

'I don't know why they keep on giving you all this home-work. I never did all that when I was at school. It'll turn your brain, if you keep on stuffing all that into it.'

'Look, Mom,' I said sniffing, 'it won't. It's the same for everyone.'

'And you'll have to have a hot-water bottle tonight. That cold's bad.'

'Yes. I will. I'll make it myself.'

'No, you won't. You'll about tip boiling water all over you if you do. Let me do it.'

So there it was. I took to my bed with a muzzy head, dreaming of scalding water splashing all over me. I wasn't surprised when in the morning I felt horrible. No one can say I'm an early riser, but I usually look forward to school. This morning, I felt desperate. My throat and head ached, and I felt like dying.

I spent half the day asleep. The other half I spent cursing myself for forgetting something important. The night before I was supposed to have gone with David to see Mr Reed. He was going to tell us what results his researches in the reference library had produced. We'd both forgotten, and gone wandering vaguely down the village street in the rain. It was so rude to Mr Reed!

Now I began to worry about David. Would he know what had happened to me? It was boring not to see him, too. So the time passed miserably; not content with being bored by not seeing David, I found myself wondering why this should make me bored. I had no books to read, and by mid-afternoon the scene outside was dank and overcast. I needed to put the light on to cheer me up, but dursn't because of wasting electricity. I fiddled about in my mind with the story of Abigail's last week alive, and what had made her die. Eventually I flopped out of bed and got an old Geography note book. Ruling off an unfinished page, I wrote: *What Happened to Abigail Parkes?*

Here I bit the top off my biro with the depth of my thought. The rest of the biro still worked, so I went on.

i. Abigail Parkes met David Caddick, a butty collier, in her father's kitchen.

ii. They became friends.

iii. They were talking one day at the end of a drive when Henry saw them, and put a stop to the affair, as he thought.

iv. But he thought wrong. They met in the canal tunnel, and he gave her a ring.

v. She stitched the ring into the sampler. Then she took it out again, and somehow lost it in the canal.

vi. During the last—

I broke off. A letter had plopped through the front door.

It was nearly half past four by my wristwatch. I plodded downstairs to see what had come; in our area, there is no afternoon post.

I was pretty amazed to find the writing on the outside of the letter was David's. *Miss T. Willetts*, I read. When I ripped the top off the envelope, a wodge of school rough paper fell out. Some of it was written over in biro, some in pencil. In the dark of the hall, I couldn't read a word except what was on the envelope. I ran back upstairs. Ran? —I must have been feeling better, then.

The letter started abruptly, without any *Dear Teresa*. It said:

I am sorry you are away today. I suppose you caught a cold in yesterday's rain. Do you realise we should have gone to see Mr Reed last night? I made our apologies, and he told me all about it.

In the paper, it told how Fiery Holes mine was near an old shaft blocked off because of wild fire. This used to happen at times, and there was no way of putting the fire out. As long as there was coal below the ground, the fire used to burn, feeding on the slack and small coal that had been left by the colliers. The best coal was taken away in heavy lumps, and all the rest was left; it just wasn't worth while getting it out. The only way they could stop the fires was to block off the gallery with something that wouldn't burn, ironstone walls, or rubble. That's what they did with Fiery Holes.

But it seems that on the Tuesday before Abigail's death the fire was beginning to break through the wall of ironstone. Someone had the brilliant idea of turning on a great jet of water and trying to put the fire out to save the rest of the mine. It was a silly thing to do, because when the water reached the fire, fumes and steam resulted and swept back through the mine gallery, where the colliers were still working.

The next day's paper reported the names of the miners overcome by the fumes, scalded to death by boiling water and steam, etc. Altogether there were seven. David Caddick was the butty in charge, and he was listed too.

'Yes,' I thought, 'but that's impossible. How could David have fished Abigail's body out of the canal on December 10th when he'd already died, overcome by fumes and choking, withering steam in Fiery Hole mine? Surely Abigail knew about the disaster?'

Do you realise [David's letter went on] that this means Abigail thought David Caddick was dead? Even if her father didn't tell her about the mine disaster, it was only a few fields away. And she'd read the names of the dead in the paper. There's no wonder she committed suicide, really.

I put the letter down. How should I know whether he was right or not? How could anyone *know* what it's like to hear that someone you love has been killed so horribly, unless it has happened to you? I tried to feel this; but feeling wouldn't come. Abigail might have been driven crazy; she might have thought life wasn't worth living. Love might be like that. Shock might be like that.

The letter went on:

On Thursday the paper said the fire could not be brought under control. The pit would have to be abandoned. The bodies of three men had been brought up, but the others could not be reached.

Henry Parkes must have known that David Caddick wasn't among the dead. We know from the inquest he set him on straightaway at Black Bank. He was a butty, remember, directly employed by Henry. He must have known that Abigail was overcome with grief about the disaster, but he never even told Susanna that her brother had been listed by mistake, or whatever it was. He deliberately didn't want Abigail to know, but let her stew in her own juice. That's Victorian, if you like.

'And that's another reason why he'd be so keen at the inquest to show she didn't commit suicide. He'd have had it on his conscience for ever,' I thought.

The letter finished:

And the rest of his life he kept in touch with Susanna, trying to prove to himself that he hadn't driven his daughter to suicide, and his first wife into a decline. It makes sense.

I hope you'll soon be better,

Yours sincerely,

David H. Ray

I still felt ill on Wednesday. It wasn't till Thursday that I returned to school, still sniffly. David greeted me happily, but a bit shyly. Then to my great suprise, he honoured me with an invitation to tea on Saturday. Albion was at home, but neither Val nor Dad was going. In any case, Val and I were still at daggers drawn. But it wasn't only friendship that had prompted Dave to ask me to tea.

'I want to explore the canal tunnel,' he said. 'Have you thought about it? The more I think, the more I feel sure they met there.'

'That means you believe what I heard in the tunnel,' I exclaimed, overjoyed.

He looked at me very kindly. 'Yes,' he said. But I have no idea from that day to this whether he really did believe me, or whether he felt he must trust me, or what.

'I've got an idea there must be something in there to discover.'

'Discover?'

'Things are getting clearer, you see,' he explained, over our usual vending machine drink. 'We know Abigail had been given this ring by David Caddick, perhaps at their secret meeting place in the canal tunnel. First she stitched it into the sampler, then she wore it. Remember what Susanna said at the inquest?'

'A bit cheeky, wasn't it, in full view of her father?'

'It was. Perhaps she hid her hand when he was near.'

'She had to keep it, at the end, to remind her of David; she thought he was dead.'

'And that's why she committed suicide, if she did.'

'But I tell you she didn't,' I insisted.

'But what she did do, we'll never know.'

'I feel I shall know, one day,' I answered.

'She had a good motive.'

'But feeling suicidal isn't the same as doing it. Your vicar told me that. He reckons he feels suicidal about the people singing on Sunday, but so far he hasn't thrown himself off a canal bridge.'

'That's a joke, though. Listen, Tess. That ring. Last night I was talking to Mr Cutler—the gravedigger, remember? He told me people in Victorian times, and still today, liked to be buried with their rings on. The rings stood for eternity, you see. They must never be parted from their rings even in death.'

'Good Lord!'

'But it looks as if Abigail's ring fell off before that. And now your Jean's got it. That's odd.'

I could not put into words the ideas that came to my mind about the ring which must always remain united to Abigail and which had become parted from her, nor could I understand which was Abigail, the body in the churchyard, the ghost at the bridge, or the remote relations who lived in our council house in a totally different age. Body, ghost and living girls, in some sense all seemed to partake in her nature.

'The odds against your Jean getting the ring back must be enormous,' David went on.

'By chance, yes,' I said. 'But it wasn't chance. Anyway, so what do you hope to find in the tunnel?'

'I don't know. But it would be a grand secret meeting place. I don't see why I shouldn't trust your intuition, or whatever it is. It does fit the facts. There may be something, even if it's only initials scratched on the wall. I shall find something.'

'Why the canal tunnel as a meeting place?'

'Safe as anything. No one'd ever go looking for them down there. And if they did, there'd be plenty of warning.'

'They'd be trying to prove their love would hold despite the whipping, I suppose,' I said.

'Absence makes the heart grow fonder,' he said cryptically. 'And with Henry saying "No" that would be a challenge.'

'And it was so important they may have marked it?'

'Yes. So let's try the tunnel on Saturday. And afterwards, you come to tea.'

And so it was settled. I prayed for Saturday to come quickly; but it came in its own good time. Good things can't be hurried on, nor evil delayed.

19

Memorial in the Tunnel

For a few moments we paused at the tunnel mouth. The water gloomed away in the inside, but not far away in the tunnel it disappeared and you couldn't see it any more. What if, inside, it came over the towpath, and we drowned in blackness?

'It's like an entrance to Hell,' I said to David.

'I don't know why we're hivver-hovvering here,' he answered. 'Canal boats never do; they just go straight in. One minute you can see them, the next they've disappeared under the earth.'

'It's like going down a coal mine,' I said. 'I don't like it.' But after that, I was determined to say nothing more. David would think I was 'frit'.

We stepped inside, thankful we had a torch which we could switch on when the light faded completely. At first, daylight followed us not far away. We could see each others' faces, even the dark coats we wore. Looking back, we watched the thin film of ice on the canal surface reflecting the daylight's gleam. I picked up a pebble and tried to skim it across, but it broke the ice and fell into the depths of the water. The surface of the towpath was uneven and muddy; the blue brick edging had crumbled in places, and we tried to hug the side wall of the tunnel. This was not so easy, though, because the tunnel soon arched, and there was hardly any room to stand by the side wall. We bent down slightly, scuttling along like rabbits in a burrow, and drops of murky water dripped on us from above.

The light behind us was now growing dimmer, and I wished Dave would turn the torch on. I began to think he might be a kind of owl, that could see in the dark, and I wondered if this was an advantage of wearing glasses. I found I was running my hand along the tunnel wall to check my position. Perhaps the towpath was two foot six inches wide, but it seemed like a sheep track. We were moving mighty fast, too, and I had the sensation that my feet were detached from me and were acting automatically, not under my control.

'Dave,' I cautiously said between breaths.

He didn't hear.

'Dave!' I shouted louder, after his receding back. Again there was no answer, and I felt he was moving away from me in the deep shade of the underworld where we had ventured.

I stopped and listened. Bumbling footsteps in the pitch dark some yards ahead showed that he had not so far fallen off the path. But to tell the truth, I hardly had the power to follow him. My feet were all right, not tired or anything; but I just didn't want to go on with the expedition. I wondered what we could hope to find. Bother Abigail, and the wild goose chase she was leading us! Why couldn't we be content with finding the inquest report? What did it matter whether she had committed suicide or not? Who cared? She seemed to be pursuing us like a hound pursuing his quarry, driving us into danger and fear amidst the terror of the dark and the listless water.

'Dave!' I bellowed, as loud as I could.

The footsteps stopped.

'What's the matter?' I heard his croaky boy's voice say, muffled in the confined space.

'Wait for me. I can't catch you up. You're going like a jet plane. I can't see a wretched thing.'

'You don't need to see,' he answered. 'Just keep hold of the tunnel wall.'

'I was thinking you could see in the dark, like an owl.'

'No. I can't see at all in here. But as long as you keep by the wall, you're all right.'

I stumbled on to catch up with him. In a few yards I crashed into him, and we both tottered, grabbed each other, leant away from the water towards the tunnel side, and ended sprawling in the mud. My foot trailed in the canal, which was not covered with ice this far in, and I was again ready to give up. I can't begin to say how I felt, or how my eyes and throat prickled.

'We can't be far off the air shaft,' Dave said.

'Bother the air shaft. Can't we use the torch now?'

'I never thought about it,' he calmly replied. 'Of course we can.'

'Oh boy,' I thought. 'My hero! He has a torch and it never occurs to him to use it.' I was passionately angry! Perhaps he might be able to see in the dark, like a burrowing mole, but what about me? I'd thought he was different from most boys this way, but no, he still couldn't see what was plain as plain.

The yellow light was a miracle, and set everything right. With it we could see the damp blue bricks arching over for the roof, the pools of water ahead spreading over the uneven towpath, the gloomy canal, dark green in the torch-light, with no sign of life in it so deep in the dark: no water weed, no rushes, no fish—just treacly dark liquid without a ripple.

This time we went on more happily, Dave flashing the torch over the gaunt lifeless burrow. I thought of the miners, toiling below ground. It wasn't a trade I could ever have followed! No wonder they were a race apart. David Caddick and his like had been brave men, even without the fire hazard and the falling roof. I squashed the idea of falling roofs very rapidly, and shuffled behind the leader. It was not long before a grey streak of light came in view in the top of the tunnel, and a white circle like a dinner plate showed on the surface of the still canal. We had reached the air shaft.

'I'll turn the torch off; all right?' David asked. I appreciated his asking.

'OK. It's not so bad here. I vote we stop. For a bit.'

'Well, of course. That's the whole idea. We'll need to stop, to look round.'

'Can we sit down?'

'It's very wet. But I suppose we can hardly get wetter.'

'Hardly,' I agreed. 'We can't possibly.'

I squatted down on the towpath, trailing my coat in the mud. I could see the faint outline of Dave, squatting opposite. We looked like two baboons taking up our sleeping quarters for the night.

'Well, what are we going to do?' I asked.

'My idea is to look all round, for about twenty yards on either side of the air vent. It's just possible they may have left something. It may be only initials, but there may be something else.'

'Oh, I see,' I said. But I didn't really.

He shone the torch along the path. To my surprise, there was a rag-tag trail of litter stuck in the mud, and floating on the canal. Almost directly below the air shaft there were some Cadbury's chocolate papers, a crisp bag, and some floating matches. Some yards down the tunnel, further beneath Gosty Hill, some peanuts had been trodden into the ground, and footprints could clearly be seen. Sure enough, when we went to look at the walls, initials had been scratched on the bricks, and there was a heart with an arrow through it. For a second or two I was excited, till Dave said:

'That lot's not much good. Mid-twentieth-century graffiti.'

'Graffiti?'

'Writing on walls. There's lots in Pompeii. But this has no historical value.'

'The bowels of the earth,' I suddenly said. 'Would you have liked to be a miner?'

'No fear. The darkness means nothing to me; I'm all for daylight.'

'Yes. But if you had to . . . ?'

'We'd all get used to it if we had to.'

'I suppose it's good for us to come down here. We can see what a miner feels like. These disasters must have been dreadful, like the one David Caddick escaped from. And the one in the ballad he was singing about, Johnny Southern.'

'It's funny how mines always attract people. They always think there's something marvellous to be found deep in the heart of the earth.'

'So do we, Dave. We wouldn't be here else. We've only struggled in here to find something marvellous. Like when Orpheus went down to get Eurydice back in the old Greek story.'

'But he lost her afterwards. Anyway, what are you talking about? That's just a myth!'

'We are like him though,' I answered. 'Going down to the underworld to look for lost love; Abigail's love, preserved for ever under Gosty Hill, just like her body's in the churchyard.'

He laughed; but it was sympathetic laughter. Then he turned away from the graffiti.

'What we'll do is this,' he said. 'We'll search systematically along the walls, from about twenty yards west of the air shaft to twenty yards east. Try to find a hollow brick or a sign of some sort. You take the centre, where there's enough light from the air vent. I'll take the parts further into the tunnel. And for heaven's sake, don't forget the canal is two feet behind you. We don't want another canal death just exactly on the anniversary of the other.'

'The anniversary?' I queried, as I went off to tap and poke the walls beneath the shaft.

'Yes,' he called back along the tunnel. 'Don't you remember? It was December 10th 1860. Didn't you notice today's date?'

'I didn't. I don't know if I'd have come. Still, the one thing I'm not is superstitious.'

I tapped, looking for a cavity. I pushed the bricks with my hands. They were hard, smooth bricks, and they didn't yield. Even where the mortar had rotted, the bricks stayed firm.

'Not much here,' I shouted to Dave. I glanced at his shadowy figure along the tunnel. It was all very well him saying he couldn't have cared for mining. The fact was, he seemed to have no fear of this dark gallery. His feelings and mine were quite different. It struck me he could have been a fearless, patient delver in times gone by, not rattled by trouble, but calm. Where he came from though, his ancestors were probably cotton spinners or something.

This wall was hopeless, firm as a rock. Yet I agreed with David's theory that there might be something down here left by Abigail and David Caddick. I tried to picture what and how, but my imagination was played out, it wouldn't work. Not for all the credit marks in the school could I have written a story about it, not even half a page. I worried over this in my mind.

So I never heard Dave shout at first. I wasn't even concentrating on the bricks. I didn't hear anything, even Dave.

He slithered back, and grabbed my sleeve.

'Can't you hear?' he shouted down my ear. 'I keep calling. Can't you hear?'

'Sorry. I was too busy with these bricks.'

'Forget them. We've arrived.'

I followed him down the tunnel by the light of the torch.

He had taken a brick out of the wall, and we looked into the blackness behind.

'However did you find it?' I asked.

'I just kept tapping. I didn't think it'd be far from the air vent, because of the glimmer of light you get. Not much, but just enough. Then I hit on this hollow sound and I had to joggle the brick till it came out. There was no mortar round it.'

'Well, look inside. Quickly!' I shouted.

'I have. There's a little tin, all over rust. The cavity is probably a natural one. The tunnel seems to be going through rock, partly. Ironstone, I think.'

'Open the tin!' I didn't mind whether the rock was ironstone or gold-bearing quartz, I was so excited.

'We must be careful,' he said, damping my eagerness. 'The metal might have rusted right through. It might fall to pieces.'

'Yes. Be careful. But get a move on! Blimey Ann! I must know what's inside. Perhaps it's nothing to do with Abigail at all. But I know it is.'

Of course, it was to do with Abigail. As we had supposed, the two lovers hadn't given up when Henry Parkes objected. Instead they had transferred their meetings to a safe place below ground, and sealed their association for ever by the ring he had given her, and this little tin, now rusting away, which they concealed behind the brickwork in a cavity just visible by the glimmering light given by the air vent. David unwrapped his long scarf, yanking it out from the depths of his coat without undoing the buttons. The scarf was to protect the frail tin from all harm.

It hadn't occurred to me, but we found as soon as we removed the rusting top—the hinge snapped apart—that Abigail could write but David couldn't. She had put into the tin a letter, a locket, and two pieces of hair. I know people might call this Victorian sentimentality, and wonder who in their senses would go and put bits of hair in a tin in a canal tunnel. And all I can say is that folk are senti-mental, not just Victorians. As I looked at these pathetic relics, I knew I would be the kind of person to do just the same kind of thing and store up treasure as a token of my heart.

The hair and the locket we put by. We read the letter at once, and felt almost that we were meeting Abigail. Of all the things we'd seen connected with her, only this and the sampler were her own work. She had held this paper in her hands, and written on it, frowning over the letters in the candlelight.

The letter said:

We the undersigned do make a solemn promise of fidelity. Neither the world's disdain nor death shall part us. This casket shall be our memorial for ever if the hazards of life or death prevail. We shall hope to meet in eternity.

ABIGAIL PARKES   DAVID X CADDICK,
                                            his mark.

A shaky postscript was added:

Since my love was killed at Fiery Holes pit yesterday, I seal this memorial with my locket. His ring I shall wear all my life.
                                                                                    A.P.

As we found later, she tried to keep this promise, but failed.

Wrapping the tin in the scarf again, with David clutch-ing the scarf close to his body, we began to trace our muddy steps along the towpath, back into a world of ice and hazy sunshine.

20

Suicide Disproved

Even before the photo album, I was in Abigail Parkes' power. But since I had found out my blood relationship to her, I had felt more and more certain of her influence over me. Generally I felt the influence friendly, but always mysterious and just at times frightening. From the first moment I knew her, I had felt responsible for correcting the coroner's verdict; for I was sure it was untrue. This had become a crusade, as the vicar had said. Otherwise I should never have ventured under the hill with David.

As I shuffled back along the towpath, I wondered what the new discovery meant. It proved that Abigail thought David Caddick was dead, buried in the rocks of the mine, or roasted alive. It seemed to drive me still nearer to believing the suicide verdict, against my own will. I thought of Susanna's evidence, and how she had said 'You remember the mine disaster, sir?' But I thought of other evidence, too, that pointed the other way.

'Daylight ahead,' David suddenly shouted.

'Thank heavens for that,' I replied, my mind still occupied with the coroner's court.

We emerged into the frosty world outside. Leaves were outlined in white, pools were covered as though by polythene sheeting, the canal's coating of ice seemed to have strengthened. Again I was tempted to skim a pebble across the frozen cut. Again it fell through and sank to the depths, showing how thin the ice was.

'I can hear a train,' said Dave. 'Let's go and look.'

We went beneath the bridge and stood by the roadside looking back as the train pulled out of Old Hill station and over the rumbling arch.

'Only a D.M.U.,' David said wisely. 'They mostly are.'

'What the hell's a D.M.U.?' I asked.

'Diesel multiple unit,' he replied. 'All these trains from Brum to Hereford are made up of them. Not exciting.'

I don't know anything about railways, but I could add my little bit.

'Dad used to go to work from the station here. Right to Longbridge. A good while ago, that was. Steam, of course.'

'I know the one you mean. A very pretty line through Frankley. I've seen where it used to be. But for steam, you've got to go to Bridgnorth now. Everything changes.'

'Aren't we a bit young to be moaning about everything changing?'

'Not where steam's concerned. I wish I'd lived in those days.'

'Was this railway line here in Abigail's day?' I asked.

'Not till a good while after.'

'Well, then. I wish I'd lived in the days before steam ever came to Old Hill. I wish I'd been here to see what happened on December 10th, 1860.'

I took a comb out of my school blazer pocket and began to comb the hair out of my eyes. (Since the churchyard time I knew not to dress up for David.)

'I suppose we'd better go back home,' he said.

'Just a tick,' I answered, my comb poised in my hand and a note of urgency in my voice. 'Look at Wright's Bridge. That woman on the top with the maxi dress. What's up with her hair?'

The young woman's hair was blowing about, all dishevelled in the wind. Yellow-gold it streamed out behind, then fell over her face and covered her cheeks. But the thing was, that where we were standing, there wasn't any wind. Freak weather I have heard of, but this was beyond mere freak.

I felt Dave clutch my elbow, worried, I suppose, by the oddness in my voice.

'What ever . . . ?' he whispered.

'Hush, oh hush!' I breathed back. And then, my lips barely moving, 'It's her.'

It was just as the old miner had told the coroner. Abigail was standing on the centre of the bridge, fidgety and wind-tossed. All was the same, except that it was broad daylight, and our weather was quite still.

I was lost entirely, my heart on the bridge with Abigail. But I had an impression too of David's face, watching mine in tense concern, trying to guess through the barrier of communication what was happening to me. Silently he guided me round the railings to the side of the bridge where Abigail was standing, now shaking her head impatiently, now staring down at the dark water, nervously fiddling with her buttons or the ring on her finger. It was uncanny to see her there in calm daylight, acting as though it was stormy night time; it seemed as though two films had been superimposed one on the other and were running at the same time, a film of the here and now and a film of Victoria's day.

I looked full at her face. I'd seen it before, of course, very close, reflected in the water on the day she had looked over my shoulder on this bridge. She could have been my sister, so like was she: she was almost Jean's twin. The photos in my nanny's album at Weston had shown me the same face; my dreams had contained the dark blue eyes, the blonde lanky hair, the thrusting chin and wide mouth. No one could have mistaken her for anyone else.

'Will she see us?' I whispered.

'I don't know,' David answered, puzzled, strained, hushed. 'I don't know anything. Let's sit down.'

'What? On the icy grass? I'm catching my death this afternoon!'

'All right. Lean against the railings. We can watch what happens.'

'Shall we see . . . ? Shall we actually see . . . ?' I queried.

'I don't know what we'll see. Could be anything. I've never seen a ghost.'

'It's not a ghost,' I put in vehemently. 'You can see how real she is. She's as real as you are.'

'Shut up, Teresa,' he said, but not unkindly. 'Leave her alone.'

I watched her lean over the bridge again and again stare at the deep water. All the while she fidgeted and fiddled; there was no calm in her. Suddenly, the ring she was toying with slid off her finger, and I heard the echo of a cry, far away, from Abigail's voice. She strained to see where the ring had fallen, the ring she had vowed to wear for ever, for 'all her life'.

It bounced on the ice! Of course, in 1860 that wasn't what happened, but now I saw it skimming and skithering as I had wanted my little stones to do at the tunnel mouth. We stood there frozen while the gold ring danced and flashed in the winter sunlight, till it disappeared from view, perhaps because it finally broke the cat ice, or perhaps because hallucinations do not last for ever. The girl on the bridge was stunned. She stopped her restless movement and peered with agonised sadness down into the water, just as I had seen her face peer over my shoulder before.

The she moved off the bridge. I remembered with force the old collier's evidence at the inquest. She moved off the bridge; he had seen her outline. Determination firmed her mouth; her sad eyes intended something. Down to the bank she walked, obstinacy fighting despair in her face. She grabbed a pole lying by the side of the canal, pushed it far into the water, and uselessly dragged it along the bottom. It was so heavy I could see her strain as she balanced precariously on the edge. It seemed as though the cat ice fractured when the pole was thrust in; I don't know, perhaps I saw wrong. Rain water dripped from her, and the far-off terrible wind blew its gusts at her from another world as she struggled there to get out her precious ring from the cut. Of course, it was absurd. You might as well fish for jack-bannocks with a pencil.

I knew now what would happen. All of a sudden the pole's weight overbalanced her, and she slipped headlong from the bank. But I didn't know the next part of the story, which was a shock and a surprise. I found myself pelting towards the water's edge, driven by a raging impulse to save her from drowning. I saw nothing but glinting blackness, but I knew where she was and I leapt for the spot. I never thought; I can't see now what made me do it. It was more foolish than Abigail's attempt to get back her ring. I hurled myself at the cat ice, which splintered around me with an eerie screeching noise. It didn't even break my fall, and I found myself, a non-swimmer, thrashing hopelessly about, as cold and desperate as I ever hope to be.

The icy cold cleared my brain. Abigail vanished from it as the water closed over my head, and I made a grab at the side. Through the water as I sank I saw the moveless, horrified face of David Ray, staring down from the towpath, and I thought of my own funeral. Oh yes! I knew I was dying. Really, David hiked me out, but in that second before he did so, I knew I must die. But I held my breath, even though I had swallowed some water. I had the instinct to live even though I was fatally sure of the end.

David told me afterwards how he knelt on the bank and snatched at my threshing limbs. By a miracle, he exerted enough force to push me against the bank, which I grasped hold of. His other hand tugged at the top of my blazer, and I felt my head break surface again. He pulled and pushed me on to the bank with savage intensity, where I was shame-lessly sick and nearly burst my lungs with coughing. David paid no attention, but dragged me away from the edge, tucked the heavy coat and huge woolly bear scarf around me, and fled down to Beauty Bank for the telephone kiosk.

21

Postscript

Since that day, I have never seen Abigail again. She's never come into any dream of mine, and except for making this record, I've never tried any Creative Writing about her. We still have the corroding tin which we found in the canal tunnel, with Abigail's note, her locket, and the strands of hair. David keeps it at his house, as I can't quite trust it not to set me off again. We've also kept the inquest report and the notes from the paper about the Fiery Holes disaster. But there's no life in any of these things now, they seem quite sterile.

The last time I saw the gravestone was at Christmas. David's family had asked me up to their house again, since I had spoiled the other time, being silly enough almost to drown to save Abigail drowning, and she long dead. For the sake of peace, I agreed to go with them up to the church for their midnight Christmas service. David still sings in the church choir, despite his croak, and I suppose later on he'll be a good tenor. I'd still much rather he sang 'folk' though, and I know he will one day.

The churchyard lay there, all mysterious under half an inch of snow. The lighted church windows cast long beams of many-coloured brightness over the sparkling white, and the graves looked like an army of resurrected people, waiting for a golden bell to ring before starting a joyful pattern of dance. One of the coloured beams of light shone directly across Abigail's grave.

'D'you mind if we go and have a quick look?' I asked.

Mr and Mrs Ray nodded their heads.

'Go on,' said Mrs Ray. 'Just you two. We'll go inside. It's too cold to stand about here.'

We scampered over to the grave, which looked just a bit jolly with a rakish cap of snow on it.

'You see,' I said. 'Henry Parkes was right after all in getting her buried in the main churchyard. And Mr Ward needn't have looked so worried, as he did in my dream.'

'*Innocent of all harm,*' read David. 'But only just. She nearly had you buried up here as well as herself.'

I was going to say, 'And I bet you'd never have bothered with any winter wild flowers,' when I felt that took too much for granted. Things I didn't want taken for granted, because they had no truth in them.

'Except you'd have been in the new cemetery,' David went on cheerfully.

'Think I'd have stayed in?' I asked. 'I'd certainly haunt you, if no one else.' That remark, I felt, expressed things better, but he didn't answer, not being flippant like me.

Inside the church it was warm and cosy. The light was rich and clear, and I don't know how it is, but the music at Christmas can get you, somehow. I thought of the light flooding out from the coloured window across Abigail's grave, and remembered how different was the miserable little torch glow on the night we'd first seen the strange words which started our quest. The howling wind and wild rain of that night had passed into eternity and been replaced by this white-gold peace; but still I saw the words *Innocent of all harm . . . Innocent of all harm* dancing before my eyes when I closed them for the prayers.

Next morning I slept late and woke to a splendid surprise. Hanging on the opposite wall of my bedroom was the sampler, with new clean glass in it, sparkling like the crystal snow outside. Mom and Dad had had it reframed as part of my Christmas present. I jumped out of bed and gazed at it, as so many times before.

How I wish I could stitch like that, such a complicated pattern, so bright and sharp in its yellows, so dark and mysterious in its blues and greens! But I'm hopeless at needlework, as the teachers have never stopped telling me. Yet I'd dearly love to make something, anything, so beautiful that it would entrance people like the sampler entrances me. One day, perhaps I will.

Heard about the Puffin Club?

. . . it's a way of finding out more about Puffin books and authors, of winning prizes (in competitions), sharing jokes, a secret code, and perhaps seeing your name in print! When you join you get a copy of our magazine, *Puffin Post*, sent to you four times a year, a badge and a membership book.

For details of subscription and an application form, send a stamped addressed envelope to:

The Puffin Club Dept A
Penguin Books Limited
Bath Road
Harmondsworth
Middlesex UB7 0DA

and if you live in Australia, please write to:

The Australian Puffin Club
Penguin Books Australia Limited
P.O. Box 257
Ringwood
Victoria 3134